"Are you saying we're now completely alone here?"

He eyed her quizzically. "You have a problem with that?"

Yes, of course she had a problem with it! Being an unwilling guest here was bad enough, but now it transpired that she was completely alone here with the dark and dangerous Dmitri!

Those earlier butterflies in her stomach began to do a tap dance. "It's not exactly an acceptable arrangement, now, is it?" she quavered.

"In what way is it not acceptable?"

Apart from her own feelings in the matter?

And had he been quite this close to her a minute ago? Lily wondered nervously as she suddenly found herself gazing up into eyes that were now only inches above her own, allowing her to see the darker green shards of color that fanned out from the black of the iris, and the incredibly long length of his dark lashes. He possessed an earthy maleness that even now was curling insidiously into Lily's bloodstream, warming her, and at the same time making her totally aware of just how devastatingly attractive he was.

CAROLE MORTIMER is one of Harlequin Books's® most popular and prolific authors. Since her first novel, published in 1979, this British writer has shown no signs of slowing her pace. In fact, she has published more than 170 novels!

Her strong, traditional romances, with their distinct style, brilliantly developed characters and romantic plot twists, have earned her an enthusiastic audience worldwide.

Carole was born in a village in England that she claims was so small that "if you blinked as you drove through it you could miss seeing it completely!" She adds that her parents still live in the house where she first came into the world, and her two brothers live very close by.

Carole's early ambition to become a nurse came to an abrupt end after only one year of training due to a weakness in her back, suffered in the aftermath of a fall. Instead, she went on to work in the computer department of a well-known stationery company.

During her time there, Carole made her first attempt at writing a novel for Harlequin®. "The manuscript was far too short and the plotline not up to standard, so I naturally received a rejection slip," she says. "Not taking rejection well, I went off in a sulk for two years before deciding to 'have another go.'" Her second manuscript was accepted, beginning a long and fruitful career. She says she has "enjoyed every moment of it!"

Carole lives "in a most beautiful part of Britain" with her husband and children.

Other titles by Carole Mortimer available in eBook:

Harlequin Presents® Extra

Harlequin Presents

*The Lyonedes Legacy

Carole also writes fast-paced Regency romances
for Harlequin Historical!

A NIGHT IN THE PALACE

CAROLE MORTIMER

~ A Christmas Surrender ~

HARLEQUIN®

entertain, enrich, inspire™

Recycling programs
for this product may
not exist in your area.

ISBN-13: 978-0-373-52889-9

A NIGHT IN THE PALACE

First North American Publication 2012

A NIGHT
IN THE PALACE

CHAPTER ONE

'This is an urgent announcement for Ms Giselle Barton, travelling on the thirteen-thirty flight to Rome. Please come immediately to desk number six in the departure terminal. Ms Giselle Barton—go immediately to desk number six.'

Lily Barton—no one but her dearly missed mother had ever called her Giselle!—had struggled all the way through the airport terminal, dragging her wayward case behind her to desk number fifty-two to join the long queue of people waiting to book in for the flight to Rome. She now gave a disbelieving groan at the realisation that desk number six had to be all the way back where she had originally started from.

So far on this cold December morning, only two days before Christmas, Lily's taxi had been late picking her up from her apartment, and the freezing temperatures and the snow that had been falling for most of the night had made the journey to the airport both slow and treacherous—ensuring that Lily was likely to be the very last passenger to join the queue checking in for Rome. As a consequence she would probably be allocated a lousy seat on the plane. No doubt squashed between two overweight businessmen who would spend the whole flight trying to look down the scooped neckline of her blue sweater once she had removed the heavy jacket she had worn against the freezing English weather outside!

To add to her misery, one of the wheels had decided to drop off her suitcase—an old and battered one of her mother's—as the taxi driver pulled it out of the boot of the car outside the airport. It had then refused to be fixed back into place, meaning that Lily now carried a superfluous wheel in her over-large shoulder bag—which had already weighed a ton even before the addition of the metal wheel—and the suitcase now had a tendency to veer off to the left as she attempted to drag it along behind her.

If, for some reason, she was now going to be bumped off the flight to Rome—which was highly likely considering how late she had booked her ticket and the fact that most flights tended to be overbooked at this time of year—she was just going to sit down and howl! It really would be the last straw in an already disastrous day.

'Ms Giselle Barton—please come immediately to desk number six in the departure terminal.'

'All right, all right, all right!' Lily muttered as the announcement was repeated, grabbing the handle of her suitcase to walk back to where she had started. The announcement had sounded more imperious this time, she noted, which probably meant she was definitely going to get bumped off the flight. No doubt with an offer to rebook her onto one leaving after Christmas.

Damn, damn, *damn*.

It had been a last-minute decision to spend Christmas in Rome with her brother—Felix had moved over there to work as PA to Count Dmitri Scarletti three months ago—when Lily's original plans for the holidays had fallen through. She should have known better than to think that Danny, the man she had been dating for the past couple of months, would abandon his divorced mother—with whom he still lived—in order to spend Christmas with her after Miriam had made it clear she had no intention of inviting Lily to join them. The perfect time, Lily had decided ruefully, to end that particular going-nowhere relationship.

Thank goodness her emotions hadn't been seriously involved; Danny, a fellow teacher at the secondary school where they both worked, had been fun to go out to the cinema or dinner with, but his domineering and demanding mother was a definite turn off!

Once her decision to go to Rome for Christmas had been made, Lily had felt her excitement start to grow. She had never been to Rome—or anywhere out of England, as it happened—and it would be lovely to see her brother again after all these months apart. Their parents had both died eight years ago, bringing brother and sister closer than ever, and emails and phone calls just weren't the same as actually spending time with the irrepressible Felix.

Well…it *would* have been exciting to spend Christmas in Rome with her brother, after Danny had proved to be such a disappointment, but as Lily was about to be bumped off the flight she might just have to settle for a turkey meal for one in front of the television in England. Wonderful. She *didn't* think!

The heating in the terminal seemed to be on full, ensuring that Lily was hot as well as bothered by the time she reached the other end of the building—only to stand in the middle of the cavernous and crowded terminal for several disorientated minutes as she endeavoured to locate desk six.

There didn't appear to be a desk six. Desk five, yes. And a desk seven. But no desk six—

'Miss Barton?'

Lily turned abruptly, almost falling over her own suitcase as it remained solidly in place behind her without the benefit of that second wheel. Lily blew several tendrils of platinum blond hair out of her eyes before focusing on the beautiful dark-haired flight attendant who stood up from behind an unmarked desk and towered over Lily's five feet two inches in height as she moved to join her. 'I'm Lily Barton, yes...'

The other woman eyed her uncertainly. 'Lily? But—'

'Don't worry about it—it's a family thing.' Lily had absolutely no interest in explaining that as a young child her brother, unable to get his tongue around the name Giselle, had instead called her Lelly, which had eventually become Lily. And stuck fast. Thank goodness; Giselle sounded like someone's elderly aunt. And whilst she might one day become exactly that, at only twenty-six she preferred to stick with Lily! 'See.' She fished her passport out of the zip pocket of her bag and held it in front of the other woman's beautifully straight nose.

Not the most flattering photograph ever taken of her, Lily acknowledged ruefully. Oh, her long and completely straight—and completely natural—platinum-blond hair was tidy enough, but her blue eyes had widened as soon as the flash went off, giving her a slightly startled appearance. As she hadn't been allowed to smile her face looked slightly woebegone, and her neck appeared almost too slender to support that heavy mane of hair.

'If you're about to tell me that I can't fly to Rome

today after all—' she started, stashing the passport back in the pocket of her shoulder bag, 'then I think I should first warn you that if anything else goes wrong today I'm likely to start screaming hysterically.'

The other woman's cool demeanour softened slightly. 'Tough morning?'

Lily raised her eyes heavenwards. 'Let's not even go there.'

The flight attendant's brisk, businesslike air left her completely as she chuckled softly. 'Then I'm glad I'm not about to make it any more difficult for you.'

'You aren't?' Now it was Lily's turn to look uncertain. As well as hopeful.

'Not at all. Here—let me take that for you.' The other woman took possession of the handle of Lily's suitcase before turning to walk away, somehow managing to pull the damaged suitcase smoothly along behind her as she did so. Of course!

'Hey!' Lily quickly caught up with the other woman and grasped her by the arm. 'Where are you going with my case?'

She smiled patiently. 'I'll check it in for you, and then take you through to the private lounge.'

Lily looked taken aback, then shook her head. 'I think there's been some sort of mistake.' Although it was hard to believe there could possibly be *two* women called Giselle Barton—let alone both booked on today's flight to Rome! 'I'm booked into an economy seat, which I think entitles me—if I'm lucky—to find a seat in the crowded main departure lounge.' She smiled ruefully.

The ebony-haired beauty returned that smile. 'I believe your booking was changed earlier this morning.'

'Changed?' Lily eyed her pleadingly. 'Please don't

tell me I'm now flying to Norway, or somewhere else guaranteed to be even colder than England is right now?'

The flight attendant gave another chuckle. 'No, you aren't flying to Norway.'

'Iceland? Or perhaps Siberia?' She gave a pained grimace. December had been a particularly cold month in England this year, and although Lily appreciated the temperatures wouldn't be in the twenties in Rome, it should at least be warmer than snow-covered England.

'You aren't flying to either of those two places.' She grinned openly now. 'You're still booked on the flight to Rome due to depart in two hours' time.'

'Thank goodness for that!' Lily frowned. 'Look, I realise I must seem like a country bumpkin, what with the wonky suitcase and my hot and bothered appearance, but I'm really not in need of special assistance. It's just the first time that I've ever flown—and I'm obviously making a complete mess of organising myself.'

The flight attendant chewed on her bottom lip in an obvious effort to stop herself from laughing again. 'Which is why I intend checking in for you.'

'Before taking me to a private lounge?' Lily repeated slowly.

'Yes. If you would just like to come this way…?'

Lily shook her head as she stood her ground. 'I really think there's been some sort of a mix-up. I *am* Giselle Barton, yes. And I'm booked on the flight to Rome. But I have an economy seat—'

'Not any more,' the other woman assured her briskly. 'Count Scarletti called the airline himself this morning and changed your booking to a first class seat, as well as giving instructions that you are to be given every personal care and consideration—before and during the flight.'

Count Scarletti?

Count Dmitri Scarletti?

The same wealthy and influential man, of mixed Russian/Italian ancestry, for whom Felix was currently working in Rome? Well, there couldn't possibly be two of them, could there? So it must be!

'I believe there will also be a car waiting to meet you at Leonardo da Vinci airport,' the flight attendant added enviously.

Felix was supposed to be meeting Lily at Rome airport...

Unless Count Scarletti had needed Felix to remain in his office today, rather than meeting Lily as planned, and this was the other man's way of making up for that change in their plans?

No doubt Felix would explain everything once she arrived at the apartment he rented in the city...

Lily was feeling slightly dazed from all the 'care and consideration' she had received 'before and during the flight' by the time she disembarked the plane at Leonardo da Vinci airport several hours later.

Sonia, the original flight attendant, had duly booked in Lily's suitcase, before escorting her to a completely private lounge set aside for VIPs. Which—upgraded or not—Lily certainly wasn't!

Once in the lounge she'd been plied with drinks and food by yet more attendants, before being personally escorted onto the plane by one of them only minutes before the flight was due to take off. She'd been shown to her first class seat—with not an overweight businessman in sight!—and then given champagne and canapés until she couldn't eat or drink any more. The result being that she had dropped off to sleep after her third glass of champagne, and hadn't woken up again until the plane had landed.

And if she had thought her personal—and, she admitted, slightly embarrassing—service to be over once she was outside, then she was sadly mistaken. As soon as she stepped out into the arrivals terminal she saw her name written on a card being held up by a tall and heavily muscled man dressed in a chauffeur's uniform—a man who looked more like a bodyguard than a chauffeur!

After introducing himself only as Marco, and ensuring that she was indeed Giselle Barton, he then proceeded to lift her heavy and broken suitcase as if it weighed nothing at all, before carrying it outside to a limousine parked in the 'No Parking' zone, leaving Lily with no choice but to follow him.

Her attempts to ask him questions, in a mixture of very bad Italian and English, didn't go well. Only the mention of Felix's name and Count Scarletti's received a terse 'si' of response as Marco ensured Lily was comfortably seated in the back of the limousine before slamming the door firmly behind her and moving to place her case in the cavernous boot of the car.

All of this was being watched by several dozen pairs of curious eyes, as people obviously wondered if the woman with the long silver-coloured hair, dressed in faded blue denims and a heavy black jacket, was some sort of celebrity. Obviously a celebrity who bought her clothes from a thrift shop!

By the time Marco slid in behind the wheel of the long black car to drive smoothly away from the kerb and enter the stream of traffic, Lily was flushed with embarrassment, and the glass partition separating the front and the back of the limousine wasn't conducive to any further attempts to question the chauffeur, either.

Left with no other choice, Lily chose to sit back in her leather seat and enjoy the scenery outside as the car sped towards the centre of Rome; if she was going to wake up from this Cinderella-like transformation any time soon then she might as well enjoy what was left of it!

She had been right about the temperature: it wasn't exactly T-shirt weather outside, but it was definitely ten or so degrees warmer than England, with no snow in sight. And the sun was shining too, which made everything look so much brighter and warmer. Lily was so enthralled by the city of Rome that after the first couple of near misses with other cars, as drivers honked and gesticulated, only to be completely ignored by the stoic Marco, she decided it might be best to return her attention to the amazing scenery outside the window.

Every street corner seemed to have statuary, a fountain or a nativity scene—it *was* almost Christmas, after all—along with imposing museums that easily rivalled the history of the sludge-covered London Lily had left behind her only hours ago. Many of the outside cafés were open for business too—even if the patrons had to wear coats and scarves in order to keep warm.

No wonder Felix had so obviously fallen in love with the city. And not only the city, apparently; he had informed Lily weeks ago that he was going out with a young Italian girl named Dee, whom he wanted to introduce to her at the earliest opportunity.

Rome appeared to be a city where it would be all too easy to fall in love...

* * *

Lily frowned her confusion when, half an hour or so after leaving the airport, Marco didn't stop the car outside an apartment building at all, but instead parked outside two imposing wooden doors, at least fifteen foot high. They slowly opened, and Marco then drove the car into the courtyard of a magnificent building that must surely once have been a royal palace.

The tall wooden doors had closed firmly behind them by the time Marco got out of the car and opened the back door for Lily.

Despite the teeming rush and bustle of the city outside, it was strangely silent inside these four walls as she slowly stepped out into the shadowed courtyard. Silent and intimidating. Eerily so.

Lily pulled her jacket more tightly about her as she turned to the chauffeur. *'Mi scusi, signor—parla inglese?'*

'No,' he answered abruptly, before moving to the back of the car to remove her case from the boot.

Obviously not the talkative type, she acknowledged ruefully. Which was of absolutely no help to her at all!

She realised that all the attention at the airport in England, and on the plane earlier, had lulled her into a false sense of security. She had, in fact, left Leonardo da Vinci airport with a man she didn't know and who had hardly spoken a word to her after telling her his name. And it was she who'd mentioned Felix and the Count's names, not Marco! Added to which, Lily had now been delivered to a building that looked as if it might once have been a palace but could just as easily have been a brothel! An expensive and exclusive brothel, obviously, but a brothel nonetheless.

Pictures flashed inside Lily's mind of newspaper articles she had read over the years on the lucrative slave trade in blond-haired, blue-eyed young women. Women who to all intents and purposes had simply disappeared into the ether, but who had actually been whisked off somewhere and kept locked behind closed doors, their bodies used and abused, until they were no longer young enough to attract the attention of the wealthy customers. When they were either disposed of or placed in yet another brothel—one whose customers weren't so fastidious regarding the age of the women they paid to bed.

She really was the country bumpkin she had described herself as being earlier! Shouldn't be allowed out on her own... Certainly shouldn't have attempted to fly to Rome on her own...

Slightly frightened now, she turned back to the chauffeur as he placed her suitcase on the cobbled stones of the courtyard. '*Signor,* I really must—'

'That will be all, thank you, Marco.'

Lily froze for the fraction of a second it took for an icy shiver to run down the length of her spine just at the sound of that husky and yet authoritative voice, before turning sharply to look up at the gallery above. Her breath caught in her throat as she saw there was a man standing in the shadows, looking down into the courtyard from the first floor. Even squinting hard into the depths of those shadows, Lily couldn't make out the man's features—was aware only of an impression of height and leashed power.

The brothel master, maybe?

Oh, good grief, Lily, she instantly admonished herself. Of course he wasn't the brothel master—because this wasn't a brothel. There would be a perfectly sensible explanation for her having been brought here. One the man on the gallery above could obviously give her, considering that just now he had spoken in perfect, and only slightly accented English.

She turned back to thank Marco for his assistance—only for her apprehension to return with a vengeance when she realised that the chauffeur had disappeared silently into the bowels of the house while she'd stared up, mesmerised by the presence of the man in the gallery.

Which had perhaps been the intention all along? Distracting her attention, allowing Marco to disappear, and so leaving her completely alone and at the mercy of this other man?

She turned to glare up at the man on the gallery. Damn it, she was twenty-six years old, a British citizen and a teacher, with a mortgage on her small London flat and all the responsibilities that went along with those things; she certainly wasn't going to allow herself to be intimidated by a man who was too afraid even to show his face.

'Oh. My. Lord!' Lily gasped softly as the man, as if sensing at least some of her tumultuous thoughts, finally stepped out of the shadows to stand against the balustrade, looking down at her.

She had been correct about the height: the man stood at least a foot taller than her own five feet two inches. And about the leashed power—even wearing an expensive designer label suit over a pristine white shirt and meticulously knotted grey silk tie, the man managed to exude an aura of barely restrained strength. His shoulders were incredibly wide beneath the jacket of that suit, his waist tapered and his long, long legs were encased in perfectly tailored trousers.

But it was the face beneath that midnight black haircut, quite frankly, in a Roman style—that held Lily completely mesmerised. It was a harshly hewn olive-skinned face, dominated by light coloured eyes above a straight slash of a nose and sculptured unsmiling lips. His chin was square and starkly masculine in those arrogantly chiselled features.

He looked like something from one of Lily's wilder fantasies—the sort of man every woman wanted to tame and claim for her own.

He raised one black and perfectly etched brow, and those sculptured lips curved in hard amusement as he responded to her earlier gasped exclamation. 'Not even close, I am afraid, Miss Barton.'

He knew her name! 'I'm afraid you have the advantage over me, *signor.*'

He gave a terse inclination of his head before walking towards the staircase leading down from the gallery into the courtyard. 'If you will just wait there, I will come down and introduce myself—'

'No!'

He came to an abrupt halt at the top of the stairs, that dark and arrogant brow arched higher than before. 'No?'

'No.' Lily stood her ground, shoulders tensed, booted feet braced slightly apart on the cobbles. She refused to back down by so much as the flicker of an eyelid as she met that pale gaze in open challenge. 'You can tell me exactly who and what you are from right there.'

'Exactly who and what I am?' he repeated, in a soft and yet slightly menacing voice.

'Exactly.' Lily nodded stubbornly.

He tilted his head to one side as his eyes—blue, maybe? Or green? Or possibly grey?—raked over her mercilessly, from the top of her silver head to her small booted feet, amusement glinting as he slowly moved his gaze back up to her now slightly blushing face. 'Who do you think I am?' he finally murmured slowly. 'Exactly?'

Lily was glad that this man couldn't possibly hear her heart beating twice as fast as normal from where he stood. It was bad enough that *she* knew how nervous she was, without him being aware of it too. Her mouth firmed. 'Well, if I knew that I wouldn't have needed to ask!'

The man appeared completely relaxed as he continued to stand at the top of the staircase. 'Let me see... At the airport you climbed into a car with a man you did not know, allowing him to drive you to an unknown destination before abandoning you there—and you did all this without any knowledge as to what or who would be waiting for you at the end of that journey?' Those pale eyes had taken on contemptuous gleam now.

Lily felt the burn of increased warmth in her cheeks; she had already realised exactly what she had done, and certainly didn't need some arrogant and dangerously attractive—emphasis on the dangerous—Italian pointing it out to her so succinctly!

She scowled. 'I assumed the driver was taking me to my brother's apartment. Obviously I should have behaved with a little more caution—'

'A *little* more?' he replied disapprovingly, those dark brows low over narrowed eyes, those sculptured lips a thin and uncompromising line. 'If you do not mind my saying so, you have been naïve in the extreme.'

'As a matter of fact I do mind you saying so.' Lily glared her annoyance at him. 'And if you've brought me here with some idea of asking my family to pay a ransom before releasing me, then I think I should tell you that my brother—my only living relative—is as poor as I am!'

'Indeed?' Those sculptured features had taken on a harsh and intimidating expression.

'Yes,' Lily said with satisfaction. 'Now, just tell me who you are, and what it is you want.'

He gave a slow, disbelieving shake of his head. 'You really do not have any idea, do you?'

'I know one thing—which is that I'm becoming increasingly irritated at your delaying tactics.' Her hands were tightly clenched at her sides. 'I also know I have every intention of going to the police and reporting this incident as soon as I'm released from here.'

His eyebrows quirked. 'Then it would seem not to be in my best interests to release you, wouldn't it?'

Lily had realised that as soon as the threat left her lips! 'I don't think my request for you to tell me who you are and where I am is unreasonable.'

'Not at all,' he drawled. 'I am Count Dmitri Scarletti, Miss Barton.' The darkness of his hair shone blue-black as he gave a terse nod of greeting. 'And you are currently standing in the courtyard of the Palazzo Scarletti.'

Oh.

Her brother's employer.

The same man who'd arranged for her to be looked after so well up until now.

And Lily had just repaid him by hurling accusations of kidnap and threats of arrest at him!

CHAPTER TWO

IF the circumstances had been any different then Dmitri might have been amused by the stunned dismay on Giselle Barton's delicately lovely face as she digested what he had just revealed to her. As it was, the present circumstances were such that he couldn't find any humour in anything a single member of the Barton family did or said. Even one as unexpectedly lovely as Giselle had proved to be...

Dmitri didn't take his gaze off her as he descended the staircase, sure that he had never seen hair of quite that colour and silky texture before—so pale a blond that it shimmered silver in the sunlight, and of such a length and thickness that it would tempt a man into winding it about his fingers as he pulled her ever closer...

Her eyes, stormy at the moment, were nevertheless the colour of the sky on a clear summer's day, her nose was small and straight above a perfect bow of a mouth that had surely been designed for a man to kiss and savour, and her chin was small and stubbornly pointed as she frowned at him.

He couldn't see her figure properly beneath the bulky jacket she wore over a blue sweater, but her legs were slender and yet shapely in the fitted and faded jeans, and her feet appeared small even in those unbecoming boots she was wearing. Yes, Giselle Barton was far lovelier than Dmitri had anticipated. Or particularly wished for.

At thirty-six years of age he knew that over the years he had acquired something of a reputation—both in business and in his personal life. He was a man, in fact, who publicly always had a beautiful woman clinging to his arm. A man who, under different circumstances, would have found this woman's ethereal beauty and air of independence something of a challenge. As it was, he had far more important things to concern himself with than her surprising and delicate loveliness. Indeed, her undoubted beauty was a complication he could well have done without!

The slenderness of her throat moved as she swallowed before speaking. 'I— You— It would seem that I owe you an apology, Count Scarletti.' The blush on her cheeks was obviously caused by embarrassment now. 'I simply had no idea—your chauffeur gave me no explanation—'

'He was instructed not to do so,' Dmitri interjected.

Those sky-blue eyes widened as she looked up at him uncertainly. He stood only feet away from her now, and the top of her silver-blond head didn't even reach up to his wide shoulders.

'He was?'

'Yes,' he confirmed as bent down to pick up her battered suitcase before straightening and walking towards the *palazzo*. 'If you would like to follow me, I have some hot refreshment waiting for you inside.'

No doubt this seriously attractive man could crook a finger and she would follow him anywhere, Lily acknowledged disgustedly. Except he hadn't even attempted to do that; he just expected—no, *demanded*—that Lily follow him inside.

Having already made something of a fool of herself today, Lily had no intention of continuing to do so. She made no effort to follow him, but instead made a demand of her own. 'Where's Felix?'

Those broad shoulders stiffened beneath that perfectly tailored jacket as the Count came to an abrupt halt in the doorway. He slowly turned to look at her, heavy lids narrowed over the eyes Lily had discovered only seconds ago were, in fact, a pale and unfathomable green. A pale and *mesmerising* green, actually. As mesmerising, in fact, as the rest of him.

Up close—if not personal!—Lily could see that he was younger than she had first thought—probably aged somewhere in his mid to late thirties—with a ruthless cast to those wickedly handsome features that must make him formidable in the business world, and pretty scary in his personal life too. She certainly wouldn't like to find herself on the wrong side of him...

He looked down the long length of his aristocratic nose at her. 'That is an interesting question.'

Lily gave a start. 'It is?' A frown appeared between her eyes. 'Has something happened to him?' She walked quickly across the courtyard to look questioningly into Count Scarletti's face. 'Please don't say he's been involved in a accident!' As she had already discovered, driving in Italy could be seriously hazardous to your health!

Dark brows rose over those cold and narrowed eyes. 'The answer to your questions would appear to be, *I have no idea* and *not yet*,' he rasped, with a chilling softness that sent a shiver of apprehension down her spine.

'But—I don't understand!' Lily had to take two steps to one of his much longer strides as he stepped into the cool hallway of the *palazzo*.

She faltered slightly, totally overwhelmed by her surroundings as she took in the magnificence of the marble floor and cut-glass chandelier hanging down from a cavernous ceiling overhead, the antique furnishings and obviously original paintings on the walls adding to the air of wealth and grandeur.

And it was so quiet—not a sound to be heard except the echo of their footsteps as Lily belatedly followed the Count as he walked down the marble hallway before disappearing into a room at the end of the long corridor.

Admittedly this was a huge house—palace!—and as far as Lily knew only Count Scarletti and his sister, Claudia, lived here, but even so surely there should be a feeling of there being other people in the house? Servants to keep such a huge house clean and dust-free? Others preparing this evening's dinner for their *padrone* and his young sister? Instead there was just a hollow, eerie silence…

Lily hurried to follow the Count down the hallway, and into the room—only to come to an abrupt halt just inside the door as she found herself in a room so elegantly beautiful it made her gasp softly in awe. The walls were gleaming white, with gold—real gold leaf?—picking out the intricacies of the cornices and scrollwork, and another beautiful glass chandelier hung from the middle of the ceiling. A deep blue Aubusson carpet covered most of the marble floor space, and the furniture was obviously from the early nineteenth century—delicate and lovely, with numerous expensive china figurines adorning it. Yet more original paintings were on the walls, and huge, almost floor-length windows looked out onto the magnificence of Rome's skyline.

And in the midst of all this elegance stood Count Scarletti, very tall and imposing, beside an ornate fireplace in which a fire crackled and flamed, adding a warmth to this beautiful room that Lily felt was singularly lacking in its master.

She huddled into her jacket as she felt another chill run down the length of her spine. 'You were about to explain why Felix didn't meet me at the airport as planned.'

He slowly quirked one dark and arrogant brow. 'Was I?'

Lily looked puzzled. From the little Felix had told her of his employer she'd gained the impression Dmitri Scarletti was a hard taskmaster but a fair one, expecting no more of his employees than he did of himself. In fact, she had got the distinct feeling that her brother's boss worked as hard as he was reputed to play. Certainly Felix had said nothing about the other man being cold and withdrawn and less than helpful!

She drew in a sharp breath. 'You—'

'Perhaps you would care to pour the tea before we continue our conversation?' He indicated a silver tray on the low, ornate white coffee table on which a teapot and cups had been arranged.

No, Lily would *not* care to pour the tea; she wanted to know where Felix was, and why he hadn't met her at the airport—and she wanted to know now! Except good manners—and her brother's employment by this man—dictated that she not be so obviously rude to him. Especially as the Count had taken the trouble to upgrade her to first class on the flight over here, as well as sending his own chauffeur to meet her at the airport!

Dmitri might almost have smiled at the battle for good manners so obviously going on inside Giselle Barton's beautiful head. Almost. But until he had ascertained exactly how much she knew about her brother's present behaviour he intended to treat her with the same suspicion with which he now regarded Felix.

'I am sure you must be in need of refreshment after your flight, Miss Barton.'

'Not really. I had more than enough champagne to drink on the plane,' she admitted ruefully.

'Indeed?' Dmitri drawled with obvious distaste.

Colour warmed those pale cheeks as she shifted her shoulders uncomfortably. 'Courtesy of your kindness in upgrading my seat.'

'It was the least I could do,' Dmitri said curtly.

'Yes. Well. I appreciate the kindness.'

She looked awkward, as if she were unaccustomed to such attentions. Which she probably was; Dmitri knew from his conversations with Felix these past few months that his parents were dead and his only sister lived alone in London.

'Now, I'm sure I've taken up enough of your time, so if you wouldn't mind arranging for a taxi to take me to Felix's apartment?'

'Later, perhaps.' Dmitri moved with the intention of sitting in one of the wing-backed armchairs beside the fire, and became instantly aware of the way she took a wary step backwards. Perhaps he deserved that; normally a man of cool and rigid self-control, he realised at the moment he was only barely managing to hold his inner feelings of anger in check.

An anger Giselle obviously sensed even if she didn't know the reason for it.

If indeed she *truly* didn't know the reason for it...

At the moment the two of them were playing a cat and mouse game, neither revealing to the other what they knew of this situation, but instead using the dictates of good manners as a shield to what they were really thinking and feeling.

Whatever the outcome of this conversation, she would not be leaving Palazzo Scarletti until Dmitri had decided she would.

He sat down, eyeing her mockingly as he crossed one elegant knee over the other. 'Even if you would not like one, perhaps you would not mind pouring a cup of tea for me?'

'I— Yes, of course.' She dropped her shoulder bag awkwardly to the accompaniment of the muffled sound of a metal clunk as it hit the carpeted floor. 'The wheel that dropped off my suitcase earlier this morning,' she explained with an embarrassed grimace.

Dmitri stood up smoothly. 'If you would care to give it to me...?'

Lily stared down at that lean and elegant hand for several seconds, imagining how that olive hue to his skin would look against her much paler—

Her cheeks began to burn as she realised exactly what she was doing. This was Count Dmitri Scarletti, for goodness' sake! A mega-rich and successful man, reputed to escort only beautiful and successful women. Lily—only passably pretty and a mere schoolteacher— would be of no interest to him, so any fantasies she had were a complete waste of her time!

She bent her head to hide her blushes, before sitting down on her haunches beside her bag. 'It's completely broken, I'm afraid.' Nevertheless, she held the wheel out to him; he possessed such a compelling arrogance it was impossible for her not to do so.

It was a compelling arrogance she realised was totally merited as he tilted her suitcase to one side before reattaching the wheel with a mere sideways twist and then a click.

She felt totally inadequate. Damn it, she had struggled all day with that suitcase, and in only a matter of seconds he had fixed it! 'Thank you,' she murmured as she moved to pour the tea, at the same time completely aware of his every move as he strolled across the room to resume his seat by the fire.

'You're welcome,' he answered softly.

Lily avoided his penetrating gaze as she handed him the cup of tea she had just poured—careful not to so much as touch his long and elegant fingers as he took the saucer from her. She was already completely aware of this man, without the need to physically touch him.

Although she would think that plenty of women had enjoyed indulging that need…

Those spectacular good-looks aside, there was an aloofness to Dmitri Scarletti—an emotional distance that would challenge women as well as tempt them. Not Lily, of course; she could behave impetuously—as this sudden decision to spend Christmas in Rome with Felix proved—but she wasn't stupid. Men like this one, indecently rich and dangerously handsome, weren't attracted to lowly teachers from England. Except maybe as a casual bed partner, of course, and she had always preferred not to involve herself in meaningless physical relationships.

What on earth was she *doing*?

Lily sat down abruptly in the armchair on the opposite side of the fireplace to Dmitri Scarletti, still avoiding looking at him, slightly dazed by the continuation of her wild imaginings about him.

Best she stayed only long enough find out exactly where Felix was before leaving for her brother's apartment—with or without Dmitri Scarletti calling her a taxi—and then hopefully there would be no reason for seeing the Count ever again. Lily certainly shouldn't be allowing herself the indulgence of finding such a totally unattainable man in the least attractive!

She straightened. 'I really do appreciate your kindness earlier today, Count Scarletti—'

'Dmitri. I would like for you to call me Dmitri if I may be allowed to call you Giselle?' he expanded.

Lily looked across at him blankly. 'No! I mean—' She waved her hand as she hastened to explain. 'Everyone calls me Lily.'

'Indeed?' Once again those midnight-black brows rose to his hairline. 'Why?'

'It's a long and boring story, and really one not worth wasting your time hearing,' Lily dismissed.

'I have no other commitments today,' he drawled softly. 'And surely it is for the listener to decide whether or not a story is worth hearing?'

'By which time they've already been bored silly.' Lily grimaced as she sat forward to pour herself a cup of tea after all; if the Count was in no hurry to finish this conversation—and he obviously wasn't—then she might just as well drink some tea too. It might also help to stop her hands shaking…

Intimidated was only one way of describing how this compellingly handsome man made her feel. And from a woman used to dealing with a self-opinionated headmaster and condescending male colleagues, that was quite an admission.

But as well as the man's obvious wealth and confidence there was a—a— The only way Lily could think to describe it was a *waiting* quality about this man—almost like that of a large and stealthily confident predator watching his small and decidedly vulnerable prey.

Well, she might be small in comparison to him—in comparison to most men, actually—but she certainly wasn't vulnerable. She was a woman used to keeping a classroom full of sixteen to eighteen-year-old boys and girls in check, and Lily couldn't allow herself to show any such weakness!

'Please continue,' the Count invited smoothly.

'It really isn't very interesting,' Lily insisted.

He shrugged those powerful shoulders. 'As I said, I have no other commitments today.'

That was hardly the point, now, was it? Lily just wanted to see Felix, so that they could go off and spend Christmas together. Talking of which… There wasn't a single decoration, let alone a Christmas tree, in this elegantly beautiful room to show that Christmas Day was only two days away. Didn't they celebrate Christmas in Italy? But of course they did—they just called Father Christmas Babbo Natale instead. So maybe it was Count Dmitri Scarletti who didn't celebrate Christmas?

And maybe Lily was just allowing her thoughts to wander in this haphazard way because she really had no inclination to share any personal details about herself with this arrogantly aloof man?

'Fine,' she bit out tersely, glad she hadn't bothered to explain the name thing to the flight attendant earlier; twice in one day was just too much! 'My mother named me Giselle after her favourite ballet, but it soon became obvious that the name was too difficult for Felix to get his tongue around. His version of it came out as Lelly, later shortened to Lily. I've been known as Lily ever since. Which is probably just as well, because after only two ballet lessons at the age of six it became perfectly obvious that I have two left feet! All the grace of a charging elephant,' Lily explained ruefully at the Count's questioning look.

If Dmitri had met Lily at a dinner party or other social occasion then he knew he would have found himself highly entertained by her conversation. As it was, he was far too preoccupied by other considerations at this moment to allow himself to be in the least amused by her.

'I find that very hard to believe,' he said.

'Oh, I assure you it's true.'

Dmitri slowly sat forward to place his empty cup back on the silver tray. 'Might I ask if you have heard from Felix today?'

Lily suddenly felt herself speared—yes, *speared* definitely described it!—by the intensity of that pale green gaze. Eyes that he must have inherited from his Russian grandmother, along with the sharply sculptured angles of his face and that incredible and imposing height.

Whatever, Lily felt herself pinned into place like that prey she had thought of earlier—a rabbit or a deer, caught in the headlights of an approaching car. 'I— No. Why should I have done? Our arrangements were for him to meet me at the airport.'

'Arrangements he obviously did not keep.' Dmitri coldly stated the obvious.

'Well…no. But I assumed that was because you had

needed him for something else.' Lily's earlier feelings of unease returned with a vengeance.

That silent drive from the airport, which had ended in her being brought to Palazzo Scarletti rather than her brother's apartment... The sudden disappearance of the chauffeur, Marco, once his employer had shown himself on the gallery... Dmitri's less than helpful answers to her questions... The strange and eerie silence of the *palazzo*, as if she and Dmitri were the only ones here...

Lily tensed. 'Have you even seen my brother today?'

His mouth thinned. 'Unfortunately not.'

There was an unmistakably cold and angry edge to that denial that only increased her wariness. 'Then where is he?'

'I wish I knew.' His mouth was suddenly a thin, uncompromising line, his pale green eyes becoming glacial. 'You are sure you have not heard from or spoken to Felix today?'

'Of course I'm sure!' Lily's patience was starting to wear a little thin now. 'I think I would know if I had spoken to my own brother!'

He breathed noisily down his nose, a nerve pulsing in his tightly clenched jaw. 'No text messages? Nothing at all?'

'Well, of course no—' Lily became suddenly still. 'Obviously I haven't had the chance to check for text message or calls since I arrived in Rome.'

She frowned and stood up once again to root around inside her cavernous shoulder bag for her mobile—not an easy task when it also contained her purse, a couple of paperback books, her make-up, lip salve, a pen, sweeteners and several tubes of mints! 'If you would just tell me what all this is about,' She finally found her mobile and took it out of the bag. 'Perhaps I could—'

She broke off abruptly as Dmitri suddenly surged to his feet to tower over her, before deftly taking the phone from her hand. 'Hey!' Lily protested indignantly as she once again allowed her bag to fall to the floor. 'What do you think you're doing?'

'There appear to be two messages,' he said, ignoring her obvious indignation as he looked intently at the screen of her mobile.

'Messages that are obviously meant for me!' Lily swiftly plucked the phone back out of Dmitri's long and elegant fingers.

That nerve once again pulsed in his tightly clenched jaw as his eyes glittered down at her in warning. 'You are not helping this situation by being deliberately obstructive.'

'Maybe if you were to explain what "this situation" is then I wouldn't feel the need to be obstructive!' Lily glared up at him challengingly.

Dmitri drew in a deep and controlling breath, aware that he was behaving unlike his normal cool self. His only excuse was that it had already been a long and difficult morning, and consequently he was not in any sort of mood to deal with the stubbornly unhelpful Lily Barton! 'Listen to your messages and then tell me what they say,' he instructed harshly.

Blond brows rose in surprise at his tone. 'If I feel they're anything you need to know, then perhaps I will!'

Dmitri looked at her coldly as he fought down the inclination he felt to shake this particular young woman until her teeth rattled in her beautiful head. 'Just check them, please,' he finally grated, hands clenching at his sides.

Lily swallowed convulsively before dragging her

gaze from Dmitri's to place the mobile to her ear and listen to her messages. 'The first one is private,' she informed him resentfully. It was Danny, belatedly wishing her a good time in Rome. No doubt with some idea of the two of them getting together again after Christmas. Some hopes! 'The second one is…'

Lily's voice trailed off as she realised the second message was from Felix, and had been left at nine o'clock this morning, English time. Before Lily had even left home for the airport. Except at the time she had been standing outside on the pavement in front of her apartment building, waiting for the late arrival of her taxi, with no thought of checking to see if she had any voicemail messages…

She felt herself start to tremble as she heard the urgency in Felix's tone as she listened to his message. 'Don't come to Rome, after all, sis,' he warned forcefully. 'I'll explain everything when I see you again, but just don't—*don't!*—come to Rome!'

'What the—?' Lily looked up dazedly as the broodingly silent Dmitri, standing close beside her, took the phone from her unprotesting hand and listened to this second message for himself. 'Why didn't Felix want me to come to Rome after all?' she breathed softly, uncertainly, as she saw and recognised the dangerous glitter in those pale green eyes as he glowered at her. 'Where is he?'

Dmitri snapped the mobile shut with a resounding click, his jaw tightly clenched. 'As I said earlier, that is an interesting question…'

'Then I demand that this time you answer it!' Lily insisted, glaring at him accusingly as she snatched the phone back out of his hand.

Dmitri couldn't help noticing—to his own annoyance—that her blue eyes were now the colour of sapphires. There was a slight flush to the pale delicacy of her cheeks, and the perfect bow of her lips was set in a stubborn line.

'You obviously know what's going on—otherwise you wouldn't have taken the trouble to upgrade my seat on the plane, or sent your car to collect me from the airport!'

Intelligent as well as beautiful, Dmitri acknowledged, recalling his relief when he had received the telephone call informing him that Giselle Barton was at the airport in England and was booked onto the flight to Rome. For several hours before that Dmitri had been afraid that Felix might have contacted his sister and warned her not to come here.

As it was…

'No, I would not,' he accepted abruptly as he moved to stand beside the fireplace. 'As to where your brother is at this precise moment— I have absolutely no idea.' If he knew that then he would not be wasting his time talking to the man's less than helpful sister. But, as things now stood, unfortunately she was Dmitri's only possible means of locating Felix. 'But I assure you that when I do know, I have every intention of ensuring that your brother leaves Italy immediately and is never allowed to return.'

Lily became suddenly still, her confusion of emotions nothing in comparison to the frightening chill of anger she could feel coming off Dmitri Scarletti in waves. Towards her as well as Felix.

What on earth had her brother done to incur this man's cold and no doubt deadly wrath?

Whatever it was, she had no intention of standing meekly by while this man attacked her brother—

either verbally or physically. 'You don't scare me, Count Scarletti,' she informed him, grinding her teeth together as amusement glittered briefly in the pale green gaze sweeping over her obvious slenderness and lack of height. 'Don't be fooled by appearances. I'm very proficient in kick-boxing—and I'm not afraid to use it!'

Grudging respect briefly lit his eyes and he nodded. 'When this is all over I would be happy for you to demonstrate your skill. However,' he continued ruthlessly when Lily would have spoken, 'at this moment I am more concerned in locating your brother and returning my sister to her home and family without scandal than I am in any threats you may care to make!'

Lily was totally confused now. What did Claudia Scarletti have to do with all this?

'Your sister?'

Dmitri eyed her scathingly. 'I wish I could be sure you are as innocent in this matter as you sound, Miss Barton,' he rasped harshly.

'But I *am* innocent! At least…if you count ignorance as innocence.' She frowned. 'I have absolutely no idea what you're talking about.'

'I am talking of my sister and your brother's elopement earlier today!' he thundered, his patience obviously completely at an end.

Lily blinked.

Elopement?

Felix?

And Claudia Scarletti?

CHAPTER THREE

'No!' Lily protested. 'You have it all wrong,' she continued confidently. 'If your sister has gone missing then I'm sure it must be very worrying for you. But I assure you Felix has nothing to do with her disappearance. I know for a fact that he's in love with a young lady named Dee. In fact, he's done nothing but sing her praises this past two months.'

In all of Felix's text messages and telephone calls during that time he had talked of nothing but the young lady he had met and fallen in love with since coming to Italy.

'Perhaps he had trouble getting his tongue around the name Claudia too?' Dmitri muttered morosely.

Lily blanched. 'I'm sorry?'

Those chiselled lips twisted scornfully. 'Dee is, apparently, what he calls my sister.'

Lily gasped even as she fell back a step, her hand moving up disbelievingly to her throat. What Dmitri was saying couldn't be right. Could it? Felix would surely have told her if he had fallen in love with his boss's sister. Wouldn't he?

Or would he?

If Felix had once mentioned the full name of the woman he was seeing then he and Lily both knew she would have warned him against getting involved. Told him it was insane!

Claudia Scarletti! The young and beautiful sister of one of the most powerful and wealthy men in Italy. It *was* insane. Utterly and completely. Yet, while Felix might have done some less than sensible things in his life, surely he wasn't stupid enough to have eloped with Count Dmitri Scarletti's little sister?

Only Dmitri certainly seemed to think that he was…

Lily felt her face turn deathly pale. 'Are you absolutely sure about this?'

'Positive,' Dmitri said tersely, reaching into the breast pocket of his dark tailored jacket to bring out a folded piece of paper. 'My sister left this for me.' His mouth compressed into an angry line. 'In the mistaken hope, perhaps, that I would not attempt to look for her if I knew that she was with her lover.'

Lily's hand visibly shook as she took the sheet of paper he held out to her, before unfolding it awkwardly to look blankly down at it for several seconds before handing it back to him with a grimace. 'I'm afraid I don't read Italian.' She had, however, clearly recognised the name 'Felix' written several times in the text. Oh, God!

She took a step back to sit down heavily in the armchair, her pleasure at the thought of spending Christmas in Rome with Felix now replaced by feelings of apprehension as she accepted that Dmitri Scarletti might just be right about Felix's involvement with his sister, after all.

Which was no doubt the reason the Count had more or less had her watched and herded from the airport in England to his *palazzo* here in Rome. Simply out of his desire to know if she'd had any idea of her brother's plans? Or for some other reason?

Dmitri saw to the second the moment when Lily realised that his motive for having her brought to the Palazzo Scarletti might not, after all, be out of consideration for the sister of an employee, but something else entirely. As far as he was concerned, an entirely necessary *something else*!

He grimly recalled the frantic knocking on the door of his suite of rooms early that morning, waking him from the deep slumber he had fallen into after returning only hours earlier from a less than satisfactory evening spent with the woman who until six weeks ago had been his mistress. She still, unfortunately, had hopes of reviving his interest in her.

It had been an unpleasant as well as difficult evening. Dmitri had tried hard not to be cruel in his rejection, but ultimately had had no choice when Lucia had all but tried to seduce him at the dinner table. Very undignified. Very messy. And Dmitri was not a man who enjoyed having situations like that one in his life.

Learning that Claudia had eloped during the night with his English PA had put all thoughts of Lucia out of his mind as he'd begun a thorough, if necessarily discreet search for his young sister. The note she had left for him, explaining her reasons for leaving and with whom, had filled him with cold dread, and it had been after several hours of fruitless questioning of Claudia's friends when his sister's car had been located, parked at Leonardo da Vinci airport.

The location of Claudia's abandoned car had at least allowed Dmitri to remember that Felix had requested the afternoon off work today, in order to meet his own sister when she arrived at the airport later...

Several phone calls later, and Dmitri had not only ascertained the woman's flight number but had also arranged things so that when—*if*—she arrived at the airport in England, she would effectively be completely under his protection until safely delivered to the Palazzo Scarletti.

His mouth thinned now as he looked at her from between narrowed lids. 'It would appear that the pair have been secretly seeing each other for some months, and have now decided to run away together,' he bit out.

Lily was still trying to absorb everything this man had just told her. Even Lily could see the relationship was totally unsuitable—so heaven only knew what Dmitri Scarletti thought about it! Although that wasn't too difficult to guess, when he was glowering down at her with such cold and brooding intensity.

Felix was certainly handsome enough to have attracted Claudia Scarletti's interest, and there was no doubting that he was fun too, but everything else about him was totally wrong for such a wealthy, aristocratic girl.

Felix had no money to speak of—except the wage he earned working for the Count. He hadn't attempted to buy a house or apartment when he'd lived in England, but had rented one instead. He had even sold his old wreck of a car before moving to Italy three months ago, and used public transport in Rome to get anywhere he needed to go. His family connections consisted of Lily. Admittedly she was a teacher, but at the same time she was struggling financially just as he was.

In short, Felix was totally unsuitable for Claudia— and that was obviously an opinion her older brother shared!

A frown suddenly creased the pallor of Lily's brow. 'Why secretly?'

A nerve pulsed in his tightly clenched jaw. 'What?'

This time Lily managed to suppress the cold shiver that threatened to run down the length of her spine. 'Why did Felix and Claudia feel the need to meet in secret these past two months?'

Those dark brows once again rose to his midnight black hairline. 'Perhaps because Claudia knew I would never approve of her dating my English PA?' he suggested.

Perhaps... 'Is that the only reason?'

'Is that not reason enough?' he asked coldly.

Maybe. But then again, maybe not... 'I don't know. Is it?' Lily looked up at him challengingly. 'I accept that Felix wouldn't be your first choice as a boyfriend for your sister—'

'Or my last.' His top lip curled back disdainfully.

'There's no need to be insulting!' Lily felt a flush of resentment warm her cheeks.

'No?'

'At least he isn't a criminal or a drug addict!'

'Your argument no doubt being that I should thank God for that small mercy?' He began a restless pacing of the room. Much like a big cat confined to a cage. A big cat who might lash out with lethal claws at any moment.

And at the moment Lily was the only one within striking distance...

She tried to remember the things Felix had told her about the young woman he had met and fallen in love with—apart, that was, from how 'wonderful, fantastic and innocent' she was! By innocent, had Felix meant in the physical sense or—? Good Lord! 'How old is Claudia?'

Dmitri stopped his pacing long enough to look down at her. 'As it happens, my sister will be twenty-one tomorrow.'

'Twenty-one?' Lily repeated incredulously as she stood up. 'Oh, for goodness' sake. I thought from the way you were behaving that she must be about sixteen or so instead of a grown woman!' At twenty-one Lily had already worked to support herself through her university degree and had been embarking on a course for her teaching certificate. 'Obviously she has a mind of her own.' Not surprising, if she was anything like her arrogant older brother! 'And she's definitely old enough to have decided for herself whether or not she's in love. With Felix or anyone else.'

Dmitri looked at her disdainfully. 'She has merely become…infatuated with his Englishness.' He scowled darkly. 'Felix is blond haired and blue-eyed, and—'

'My twin.'

'What?' Dmitri stared at her uncomprehendingly.

Lily gave a rueful smile. 'Felix and I are twins. Born only five minutes apart.'

Dmitri closed his eyes briefly. 'Which of you is the elder?'

'I am,' she announced.

Obviously, the two could not be identical, but Dmitri could see certain similarities in their colouring and the shape of their faces. And he had to acknowledge that at twenty-six years old Lily Barton was as beautiful as her brother was handsome…

He turned away from that fragile beauty to stare out of the window, searching for the soothing calm he always felt when looking at the majestic skyline of his beloved Roma. It was a calm that completely eluded him today, though, and he knew he would know no peace again until Claudia had been returned safely to him.

Dmitri had been fifteen years old when his mother had died giving birth to Claudia, but he had always adored his much younger sister—so much so that when their father had died of a heart attack, six years later, Dmitri had gladly accepted guardianship of her. It had not always been easy, and much of his time had been spent ensuring that her childhood was a happy and contented one—to the extent that he had put aside any ideas of marriage or a family of his own until Claudia's own future was settled.

He realised now that perhaps he should not have done so. That a wife might perhaps have helped guard him against spoiling Claudia, of indulging her as much as he obviously had.

None of which was in the least helpful in this present situation!

'Count Scarletti…er…Dmitri?'

His shoulders tensed at the husky softness of Lily's voice before he slowly turned to look at her bleakly.

She took a deep breath before speaking. 'If, as you claim, Felix has eloped with your sister, then I am sure that his intentions are honourable.'

At least Lily sincerely hoped that they were! Certainly Felix had never done anything as stupid as this before…

Crashed his motorbike when he was eighteen, yes. Dropped out of university during his first year to backpack around the world instead, yes. Telephoned Lily from Australia only three months later to ask for the fare home, yes. He had paid her back as soon as he had saved enough money from his winter season as a ski-instructor in France, though. Felix might be many things, but he was not a sponger.

Nevertheless, she had breathed a sigh of relief when, three years ago, Felix had finally seemed to shake the wanderlust from his system and settled down to take a business course before working his way up the corporate ladder to become PA to the managing director of a company in England. In turn, that had led to him coming to Rome three months ago to be PA to Count Scarletti.

Lily had always been the responsible twin—the sensible one. Always there to pick up the pieces from whatever scrape Felix had got himself into.

From the murderous expression now on Dmitri's face, just at the mention of her brother's honourable intentions, Lily realised there might not be any pieces of Felix left for her to pick up this time!

His mouth thinned ominously. 'Your brother's intentions are irrelevant when my sister is already promised in marriage to someone else.'

'What?' Lily felt a sinking sensation in her stomach.

He nodded. 'Or at least she will be. Her betrothal to Francesco Giordano was to be announced at Claudia's birthday celebrations tomorrow, at our home in Venice.'

Instead of which, she'd run off with another man! 'Could that possibly be the reason she and Felix chose to elope today?'

Dmitri drew in a sharp breath. 'Possibly.'

'Which seems to imply that Claudia isn't in love with this Francesco Giordano,' Lily pointed out.

Those pale green eyes narrowed to glittering slits. 'The betrothal has been arranged since Claudia's sixteenth birthday.'

Lily shrugged. 'Obviously she's changed her mind

since meeting Felix. And as the betrothal hasn't yet been announced there's no real harm done.'

'The Giordanos and the Scarlettis have neighbouring vineyards in the hills above Venice,' he grated harshly.

Lily's brow cleared and she eyed him scathingly. 'How romantic—a marriage made in the boardroom!' She pursed her lips. 'I simply can't imagine why Claudia would prefer to elope with a handsome Englishman who's in love with her rather than agree to an arranged marriage with your next door neighbour,' she said sarcastically.

Dmitri looked annoyed. 'You do not understand these things.'

'I understand enough!' There was no mistaking the disgust in her expression; those blue eyes glittered, her cheeks flushed and her top lip curled back in a slight sneer.

'Obviously the vineyard is not Francesco's only interest in her.' He found himself defending the arrangement—much to his own annoyance.

'I don't see anything "obvious" about it,' she challenged. 'In fact, I find it pretty obscene that you intend marrying your only sister off to some man who's probably old enough to be her father.'

'Francesco is the only son of Franco Giordano, and is twenty-five years of age. He and Claudia have been friends since childhood!' Dmitri's patience—what little he had left after the shocking events of this morning—was fading fast in the face of this young woman's insults.

'Doesn't he have an older or younger sister that *you* could marry to cement the business merger instead of Claudia?' she asked pertly.

Dmitri's nostrils flared at the obvious derision in her tone. Never, in all of his thirty-six years, had anyone ever spoken to him in the way she now did. 'Francesco is an only child,' he ground out through clenched teeth.

'Pity,' she said dryly.

'Claudia gave no indication that she was unhappy with the betrothal,' he insisted.

'I think eloping with another man the day before her engagement is to be announced might be a hint in that direction, don't you?' She arched a mocking brow.

Dmitri clenched his hands together behind his back, knowing that if he didn't he was seriously in danger of putting his hands about this outspoken young lady's throat and throttling her!

'Just out of interest, how have you explained Claudia's present…absence to Francesco and his family?' she now asked curiously.

Yes, perhaps a good shake *was* in order—even if he couldn't strangle her! 'Not that it is any of your business, but I have cancelled both the party and the announcement of the betrothal tomorrow evening with the excuse that Claudia has contracted…I believe in England you call it the mumps?'

'Very clever.' Lily eyed him admiringly. 'Not only would that make Claudia highly contagious, and so prevent Francesco from visiting, but her swollen glands would also mean she won't be able to speak to him on the telephone for several days.'

'I am pleased it meets with your approval.'

Lily looked thoughtful. 'You realise that excuse is only going to work for a limited time?'

'By which time I will have ensured my sister's safe return to her home and family.'

Lily quirked a mocking brow. 'Ever heard the saying "You can lead a horse to water but you can't make it drink", Dmitri? My implication being—'

'I am well aware of your implication, Miss Barton—'

'Oh, Lily, please,' she cut in pointedly. 'After all, we're almost related.'

Almost being the relevant part of that statement, she acknowledged. His anger was now such that he looked in danger of blowing smoke out of his ears. Or rather icy vapour, of course. Dmitri was too cold, too controlled, ever to really lose his temper in the way most people did and end up shouting at her.

Which made Lily's baiting him like this dangerous in the extreme. Except she couldn't seem to help herself. There was just something so—so arrogantly superior about this man—such an air of certainty that he was right—that she couldn't seem to prevent herself from antagonising him even further.

Sculptured lips tightened in annoyance. 'Claudia will see the error of her actions once she has returned and we have had a chance to speak together.'

'I can see it now—big, scary and dominating older brother bullying his much younger and sweetly innocent sister,' she mused naughtily.

Dark brows shot up. 'I am not sure that I appreciate being described as scary and dominating.'

'Too late,' Lily quipped, knowing *she* found his cold determination completely intimidating!

Dmitri's mouth thinned at the insult. 'I also believe that minutes ago you described Claudia as being a grown woman, old enough to make her own decisions?'

'Which doesn't preclude her from being sweetly innocent.'

'You obviously have not met my sister!' He eyed her with mocking amusement.

She frowned. 'Felix assured me that Dee is very sweet and innocent.'

'Innocent, certainly,' Dmitri agreed—hoping fervently that was still true. 'Sweet may be something of an exaggeration, however.'

'Claudia *isn't* sweet?'

He gave a hard smile. 'As syrup—until she does not get her own way.'

'Oh, dear.' Somehow Lily doubted that even-tempered and fun-loving Felix was aware of that side of the young woman he had supposedly eloped with.

'Indeed.' Dmitri gave a humourless smile. 'I should also inform you that until Claudia reaches the age of twenty-five it is perfectly within my power to disinherit her,' he explained.

Lily looked at him searchingly, realising from the coldness in those pale green eyes, and the sharp, uncompromising angles of his harshly handsome face, that Dmitri Scarletti was capable of doing exactly that. It was unlikely that there was ever an occasion on which this arrogant man didn't mean exactly what he said.

His gaze was mocking. 'Is your brother in a position to keep Claudia in the life of wealth and indulgence which she has so far enjoyed?'

Lily's cheeks felt warm. 'You know he isn't.'

'Yes,' he confirmed, without apology for his obvious insult. 'And once that becomes apparent to Claudia I have no doubt she will become disenchanted with her Englishman.'

If Claudia Scarletti really was the spoilt little rich girl that her brother described, then Lily thought that would be the case too. If Claudia and Felix were already married, it would be disastrous!

'And he will likely become disenchanted with her once he realises that she is no longer an heiress,' Dmitiri continued softly.

'I believe I've listened to your insults for long enough.' Lily picked up her shoulder bag from where she had dropped it earlier. 'If you will excuse me, I believe it's time I got in a taxi and found myself a hotel for the night.'

'No.'

She stilled and once again eyed him warily, not in the least reassured by the expression of implacability on his face. She moistened suddenly dry lips. 'What do you mean, *no*?'

He shrugged broad shoulders. 'You are a young lady, alone in Italy for the first time, and in the absence of your brother I feel, as Felix's employer, that it is my duty to offer you both my protection and the hospitality of the Palazzo Scarletti.'

Lily felt a nervous fluttering of butterfly wings in the pit of her stomach. 'And I assure you that at twenty-six years of age I'm perfectly capable of taking care of myself.'

Dmitri gave a scornful laugh. 'I did not see any evidence of that earlier at the airport, when you allowed yourself to be put in the back of a car by a complete stranger without even knowing where he was taking you.'

Considering Lily had realised exactly the same thing on her arrival here, she had to agree with that assessment. Inwardly. Outwardly it was a different matter entirely. 'Marco behaved like a perfect gentleman on the drive here. In fact, since my arrival in Italy, the only person from whom I seem to need protection is you!'

Dmitri frowned. 'You are insulting.'

'I haven't even started!' she snapped back. 'You had me brought here under false pretences, then proceeded to hurl accusations about my brother—and insulted me in the process. And now you expect me to be grateful for your offer of protection and hospitality?' She gave a disbelieving shake of her head. 'I may have been a little naïve earlier, but don't ever think that I'm stupid!'

No, Dmitri would never make that mistake where this fiery young woman was concerned. He was far too aware of the intelligence in her deep blue eyes and the authority in her tone ever to underestimate her determination of will. 'It was not merely my suggestion that you stay here, Lily,' he murmured softly. 'It was an order.'

She looked aghast. 'Sorry?'

Dmitri moved impatiently. 'Along with her letter Claudia left her mobile phone—no doubt so that I could not telephone her and order her back home,' he acknowledged grimly. 'And unfortunately, after her car was found at the airport and searched, this was found down the side of the passenger seat.' He produced a second mobile phone from the pocket of his tailored jacket.

Lily stared at the small black-and-silver phone. 'It's Felix's…'

The Count's gaze sharpened. 'You are absolutely sure?'

She nodded numbly. 'I bought it for him three months ago. As a going-away present.' It had been more a way of ensuring that Felix kept in touch with her while he was in Italy. 'If you would return it to me—'

'I think not.' He slipped the mobile phone back into his pocket.

Lily felt a return of those butterflies in her stomach,

those wings beating harder this time. 'What are you doing?' Her cheeks had paled a ghostly white.

'It is quite simple, Lily,' he said harshly. 'At the present time the only means of communication that Claudia or Felix have with either of us is by landline or your own mobile.'

'Only Felix will try calling me in England. And when he keeps receiving the answer phone message he'll put two and two together and realise I must have come to Rome, after all.'

'Felix is certainly intelligent enough to eventually work out that his first message must have arrived too late,' Dmitri agreed. 'And as I have Claudia's letter, and no reason to believe she will telephone me until she is ready, we are left only with the possibility of Felix contacting you on your mobile.' He shrugged. 'I do not suppose you are prepared to leave your mobile phone with me if you leave here?'

'Certainly not!' Lily bristled indignantly.

'As I thought,' he said blandly. 'Then it would seem that, as my sister is at this moment completely at the mercy of your brother's "honourable intentions", I should return the favour in regard to his sister!'

Lily stared up at him, not sure if she was understanding him correctly. Not sure she *wanted* to understand him if he was saying what she thought he was! 'Would you just spit out exactly what you mean?' she said nervously.

'Of course.' He bared even white teeth in a hard and humourless smile. 'Until your brother returns my sister to me, you will stay here, at Palazzo Scarletti, as my personal guest.'

Exactly what Lily had thought he meant!

CHAPTER FOUR

'You're mad!'

Quite possibly, Dmitri accepted heavily. It had been a day of shocks and frustrations. And receiving the letter from Claudia, informing him of her elopement had only been the start of the nightmare.

What had followed had been a desperate search of the *palazzo*, and then the even more futile questioning of those of Claudia's friends he was aware of. After that her car had been located at the airport, along with that damn mobile found down the side of the passenger seat—a mobile Lily Barton had just confirmed was indeed her brother's. Dmitri's telephone calls to several business acquaintances had revealed that the pair had not booked with any of the airlines flying out of Rome that day, nor did the car hire companies have any record of providing them with a replacement vehicle.

To all intents and purposes Claudia and Felix had simply disappeared.

Lily and her mobile were the only glimmers of hope he had. Felix might at least contact his sister again in the next couple of days.

Which was why Dmitri felt he had no choice but to keep her—and her mobile phone—exactly where he could see and hear them.

He wasn't in the least proud of his decision to keep her as an unwilling guest, but he was determined to find his sister and bring her home before she did something even more reckless than she already had. Before—as Lily had suggested so succinctly only minutes ago—the two of them found themselves related through Claudia's marriage to Felix!

If Dmitri found her quickly enough then he might be able to avert a complete scandal by hushing up the elopement. But a totally unsuitable marriage would be another matter entirely…

'I assure you I am not mad, Lily,' he said. 'Merely desperate.'

Lily eyed him in disbelief, still shocked by his announcement that he intended her to stay here at the Palazzo Scarletti with him—and even more surprised to hear him admit that the situation was beyond his control. The man was arrogance personified. Which meant Dmitri was either as concerned for his sister's welfare as he claimed to be or that he was as concerned for his business merger with the Giordanos as Lily had accused him of being. Only time would reveal which of those things was the true reason for his present feelings of frustration.

'I realise that in Italy you're probably considered a powerful man, but I don't believe that exonerates you from abiding by the law,' she announced.

He quirked one dark brow. 'Only *probably* considered?'

Lily's fingers tightened on the strap of her shoulder bag. 'Okay, I know you're a powerful man. In Italy and elsewhere. But even a man as powerful as you can't get away with kidnapping an English tourist.'

He appeared completely unmoved by her accusation. In fact, if anything, he looked amused by it. Lily was certain she could see laughter lurking in those pale green eyes as he answered her.

'You are not a child, Lily. Besides which, I prefer to think of you as a reluctant guest.'

'You can prefer all you like,' she shot back heatedly. 'But the truth of the matter is that if I'm forced to stay here it will be completely against my will. Something that I definitely intend to scream at the top of my lungs to the nearest policeman as soon as I get out of here,' she assured him.

The amusement faded from the pale green eyes as Dmitri looked down the length of his aristocratic nose at her. 'That would be ill-advised, Lily.'

Her eyes narrowed. 'Are you threatening me?'

'Not in the least,' he answered smoothly. 'I am merely advising against your drawing unnecessary attention to this delicate situation. Especially as I would have to countermand your own accusation towards me by levelling a similar one against your brother in regard to Claudia. Tell me, Lily, who do you think the authorities would believe if that were to happen?'

She became very still. 'Claudia would deny your accusation,' she whispered.

'Perhaps,' he said, unable to completely hide his impatience with his rebellious sister. 'But you cannot be sure of that, can you?'

Knowing absolutely nothing about Claudia other than what Felix had chosen to tell her—and today's events had shown that contained huge omissions— Lily couldn't be sure of anything. Least of all whether, if it came down to a choice, Claudia's loyalties would ultimately lie with her brother or with Felix, the man she'd claimed to have fallen in love with.

Dmitri easily read the dismay and uncertainty on her expressive face. Emotions he deeply regretted causing. But until Claudia was returned to him—hopefully unmarried—he could not afford to allow those feelings to shake his resolve. 'Cheer up, Lily,' he said gently. 'I mean you no personal harm, and I am sure that you will find the Palazzo Scarletti a far more comfortable accommodation than your brother's apartment.'

Her eyes flashed deeply blue. 'A gilded cage is still a cage!'

Dmitri sighed his frustration with her continued stubbornness. 'Why do you persist in fighting me like this?'

She shrugged slender shoulders. 'Probably because I resent your unbelievable arrogance.'

He winced at her continued honesty. Nor did he have any defence against the accusation; he *was* arrogant.

He had been only twenty-one years of age when he'd inherited the title of Count Scarletti, with all the responsibilities that accompanied it—the Scarletti business empire, the numerous properties and the servants necessary for the upkeep of them—as well as guardianship of his much younger sister.

Obviously his father had tried to prepare Dmitri for that eventuality, but neither of them had expected that day to come as soon as it had—and a twenty-one-year-old as head of the Scarletti family and its business empire had been an obvious target for business rivals, as well as for criticism from the older members of his own family. At the time, Dmitri's only means of defence had been to adopt the arrogant hauteur with which his father had previously dealt with such threats. It was a lesson that he had learnt well. Perhaps too well. But that arrogance of purpose was the only way he had known in which to ensure that the Scarletti business empire and its properties would remain firmly in his possession.

As a consequence he was unused to explaining himself or his actions to anyone—and he certainly never apologised for any of them. Business rivals and family alike would only see that as a sign of weakness on his part. Which left him with no choice now but to allow Lily to go on resenting him.

He straightened. 'Perhaps you would care to see your suite of rooms?'

Lily wanted to tell him exactly what he could do with his suite of rooms! Except it would ultimately make no difference what she said to this man: Dmitri Scarletti had decided she was to remain here at the *palazzo* as his 'guest', and she already knew him well enough to know that was exactly what was going to happen.

Nevertheless she raised her chin in challenge. 'I could just open one of the windows in my bedroom once I'm alone and scream bloody murder.'

'You could,' he drawled. 'Except all the windows in the *palazzo* are locked at this time of year, in order to conserve the central heating, and the glass is of a special thickness designed to eliminate the sounds from inside as well as out.'

Which explained some of that eerie feeling of being completely removed from the rush and bustle that was Rome. 'And I suppose the door inset into those huge wooden doors at the front of the *palazzo* is the only way in or out of here, and you need to put in a security number to open it?' Lily scorned. Her scorn turned to uncertainty as Dmitri made no reply but just continued to look at her with those pale green eyes. 'It is…?'

He shrugged. 'The *palazzo* was built in the sixteenth century. At the time those fortifications were designed to keep invaders out, but I am sure they will work equally as well in reverse,' he added unapologetically.

Unbelievable! Absolutely unbelievable!

Lily shook head. 'What about the servants here? Aren't you going to find it a little difficult explaining my presence to them once I make it perfectly obvious that I'm not staying here by choice?'

He quirked one dark brow. 'I am sure I have already mentioned to you that Claudia and I were expected to leave for our home near Venice today.'

'Yes. So?'

He gave another shrug of those impossibly wide shoulders. 'It is our custom to leave Rome at this time of year, which frees the staff at Palazzo Scarletti to depart and spend Christmas with their own families. Which they have already done...'

Which would further account for the silence she had experienced earlier when she'd first stepped inside the *palazzo*! 'What about Marco?'

'Marco has also left to be with his family, now that you have been safely delivered to the *palazzo*.'

'Are you saying we're completely alone here?'

He eyed her quizzically. 'You have a problem with that?'

Yes, of *course* she had a problem with it! Being an unwilling guest here was bad enough, but now it transpired that she was completely alone here with the dark and dangerous Dmitri!

Those earlier butterflies in her stomach began to do a tap dance. 'It's not exactly an acceptable arrangement, is it?' she quavered.

'In what way is it not acceptable?'

Apart from her own feelings in the matter?

Had he been quite this close to her a minute ago? Lily wondered nervously as she suddenly found herself gazing up into eyes that were now only inches above her own, allowing her to see the darker green shards of colour that fanned out from the black of the iris, and the incredibly long length of his dark lashes. Being this close to him, she also couldn't help noticing the sexy five o'clock shadow that darkened the squared strength of his jaw, and smell the light freshness of the cologne that he wore. He possessed an earthy maleness that even now was curling insidiously into Lily's bloodstream, warming her, and at the same time making her totally aware of just how devastatingly attractive he was.

Lily was unable to look away from his compelling gaze as she moistened suddenly dry lips. 'Some people might…misinterpret the two of us being here alone together,' she murmured.

'Like who?' Dmitri slowly raised one of his hands to lightly cup one of her cheeks.

'Stop being deliberately obtuse, Count Scarletti,' she snapped, unable to move while at the same time unnerved by his touch.

'I have already invited you to call me Dmitri,' he said. 'It would please me if you did so.'

'Strange as it might seem, I'm not particularly interested in pleasing you,' she said sarcastically. 'I'm sure there must be some woman in your life who might take exception to you being alone here with me.'

'Some woman?'

Lily's mouth tightened at the mockery in his tone. 'You're perfectly well aware of what I mean!'

'Yes, I am.' He gave a slow smile. 'And there are

no women in my life at present, Lily.' He lifted a silky strand of her hair before slowly allowing it to glide across his fingers. 'But perhaps there is a man in England who would not approve of *you* being alone here with *me*?'

Lily thought briefly of Danny, and just as instantly dismissed him; despite his belated good wishes for the holidays she knew that relationship was well and truly over. '*I'm* the one who doesn't approve of being alone with you!' she said.

'Is this colour natural?' Dmitri's gaze followed the path of his fingers as they combed lightly through the hair at her temple.

It was the very lightest of caresses, and yet it was enough to cause her breath to catch in her throat. 'What do you mean?'

He gave a slight shake of his head. 'I have never seen hair quite this colour before. Like sunlight caught in moonbeams.'

'Very poetic,' Lily muttered dryly, unnerved in spite of herself. 'And, yes, of course it's natural.'

'It is beautiful,' he breathed softly.

Lily's blood pounded hotly through her veins just at the touch of his gentle fingers. She was fully aware of both the heat and power of his body as he stood so close to her, and the aching of her nipples as they hardened against the soft material of her bra.

'Stop this right now.' Lily backed away from his disturbing touch, the air rushing back into her lungs evidence that she had actually stopped breathing for those few brief minutes of physical closeness to him. 'I have no intention of becoming some sort of—of plaything to help you while away the hours until your sister and Felix return,' she said shakily, her fingers now gripping the strap of her bag so tightly that her knuckles showed white under her skin.

To make matters worse, Dmitri appeared completely unaffected by their recent closeness as he allowed the hand that had caressed her temple only seconds ago to drop casually back to his side. 'Pity,' he murmured.

Lily felt colour warm her cheeks. 'Could you show me to my room now?'

Dmitri looked down at her admiringly. Possibly only five feet two inches tall, and likely weighing only half as much as he did, she nevertheless had absolutely no qualms whatsoever in challenging him at every opportunity. Telling him more clearly than anything else could have done that, no matter what she might say to the contrary, Lily did not feel in the least physically threatened in his presence. Not in a violent way, at least...

Dmitri had been involved with far too many women not to recognise her physical response to him; her breath had hitched in her throat, her skin had become flushed and her nipples had become a hard temptation beneath the soft material of her sweater. Oh, yes, on a physical level Lily was certainly aware of him.

Just as Dmitri was completely aware of her—much to his own surprise.

His taste had always tended towards tall and dark-haired women, with curvaceous bodies. Lily was none of those things, being petite with silver-blond hair, and possessed of a slenderness that would have tended towards boyishness if not for the firm swell of her breasts.

And yet her skin had felt like warm velvet beneath his fingertips, and her hair smelled of lemons and cinnamon—no doubt from the shampoo that she used. Her eyes were so deep a blue they were like huge lakes that a man might drown in. As for her mouth…Dmitri had never before seen a mouth quite as sensually full and perfect for kissing, the top lip slightly fuller than the bottom, and both so perfectly curved he'd briefly become lost in thoughts of having the fullness of those lips wrapped hotly about his—

Basta!

Even having such thoughts proved he was behaving just like a man in need of a 'plaything'—as she had accused him of being only minutes ago!

Except Dmitri knew that under different circumstances he would have enjoyed kissing Lily as intimately as he could easily imagine her kissing him, seeking her heated centre and drinking his fill as he tasted her with his lips and tongue and brought her to the pinnacle of pleasure.

Definitely enough!

Lily appeared to be completely ignorant of her brother's plans with regard to Claudia. In fact, her only crime seemed to be that she was Felix's sister. As such, it would be totally wrong of Dmitri to even *think* about taking advantage of the fact that they were completely alone together now.

He ran a hand through his short hair and sucked in a frustrated breath. 'If you will come with me…'

Lily followed slowly along behind the Count as he walked from the room, pulling her now-obedient suitcase—the traitor!—behind him. Whatever he had been thinking these past few minutes, the hard glitter of his eyes and grimly set jaw showed her that it hadn't been pleasant.

But then neither had her own recent thoughts been,

concerning her recent reaction to the merest touch of his fingers.

What had all that been about, anyway? Oh, admittedly the man was sinfully, wickedly handsome—temptation on legs, in fact—but the reasons for her being here with him were hardly conducive to her becoming aroused by him!

All other thoughts flew out of her head, however, as he stopped in the hallway to hold a door open so that Lily could enter ahead of him. She came to an abrupt halt in the centre of the room as she found herself in a sitting room almost as big and certainly as elegant as the one she had just left. Was this room to be her own private sitting room?

Apparently so, as Dmitri was taking her suitcase into the adjoining bedroom and placing it on the stand at the bottom of a four-poster bed that looked big enough for six people to sleep in comfortably. A slightly dazed Lily was given no time to admire the very feminine room as he opened another connecting door, turned on the light and revealed the most decadently appointed bathroom she had ever set eyes on.

The floor and walls were tiled in cream and terracotta coloured marble, with a shower unit in smoky glass in one corner of the room that also looked as if it would accommodate half a dozen people. But most exquisite of all was the huge sunken bath surrounded by potted plants, the jets along its sides making it look as if it was also a hot tub.

A gilded cage, indeed...

But still a cage, Lily reminded herself heavily, and she turned away from that decadent luxury, brushed past Dmitri and walked back into the bedroom. She sat down on the side of the bed, uncaring that everything spilled out of her handbag beside her as she dropped it on the bed.

She had been so looking forward to seeing Felix again—to spending Christmas with him, exploring the beauties of Rome with him and Dee. And instead there was no Felix, no Dee—only this man and the opulent splendour of the Palazzo Scarletti.

Oh, Lily didn't blame Felix in the least for this mess. No, in her eyes Dmitri was the one responsible for everything that had happened today. Lily hadn't known him for very long—only a hour or so—but if his overbearing behaviour towards her was an indication of the way he treated his sister, then she didn't believe Claudia had dared tell him she didn't want to become engaged to Francesco Giordano tomorrow, let alone that she was in love with someone else. He had left Claudia and Felix with no choice but to run away together today.

The whole concept of an arranged marriage in order to unite two powerful families was barbaric, as far as Lily was concerned, and now she had met Dmitri Scarletti, in all his arrogant implacability, the fleeing couple had her complete sympathy.

Yet Lily could have broken down and cried with disappointment. She'd so wanted to explore the Rome she had only glimpsed on the drive here...

'Lily?'

Her eyes glittered brightly with unshed tears as she looked across the room at Dmitri. 'Would you just go away and leave me alone now?' she asked huskily. 'I'd like to take a bath and then maybe a nap.' Possibly for the whole week of her intended stay in Rome! Or at least for however long it was going to be until this present nightmare was over!

'You—'

'Will you please just go?' Lily stood up and glared at him.

Dmitri chose to ignore the aggression in her tone as he returned her gaze. Lily was very pale now, her eyes appearing over-bright in contrast to her pallor. With anger? Or something else? Unshed tears, perhaps?

No doubt it had been something of a shock to find that her brother was not in Rome to meet her, let alone to find herself an unwilling guest of her brother's employer. Well, *ex*-employer. Felix's employment with Dmitri had come to an end the moment he had learnt the other man had secretly been seeing Claudia these past two months!

Yes, Dmitri mused, the past few hours had definitely been a nasty shock for her...

'Of course.' He nodded, preparing to leave. 'We will eat dinner at eight o'clock, if that suits you?'

She roused herself enough to eye him scathingly. 'I hope, in view of the fact that all your household staff have now departed for the Christmas holiday, that you aren't expecting me to cook it?'

Whatever her emotions might or might not have been a few minutes ago, she was obviously now back in true fighting form! 'No, I am not expecting you to cook dinner,' Dmitri assured her dryly.

'Nor breakfast and lunch, either.'

He gave a rueful smile. 'Do not worry, Lily, I assure you I am perfectly capable of preparing food for both of us for the length of your stay here.'

'Really?' she asked sceptically.

'Yes, really,' Dmitri drawled. 'I cooked for myself for the three years I attended Oxford University.'

Her eyes widened. 'You went to university in England?'

He quirked one dark and mocking brow. 'You sound surprised?'

Lily *was* surprised. She had assumed—obviously wrongly—that his archaic attitude was partly due to his having spent all his life growing up in Italy. But if Dmitri had spent three years in England then he had no excuse for not realising that things were generally done differently there. That there weren't usually arranged marriages for business purposes, for one thing. That kidnapping unsuspecting females and incarcerating them in palaces was equally frowned on, for another!

But learning that he had spent three years at university in England certainly explained why he spoke such good English. Even if Lily didn't like anything he had to say!

She looked at him coldly. 'I'm still waiting for you to leave, Count Scarletti.'

So that she could take a bath and a nap, Dmitri recalled—and was instantly assailed with imaginings of how Lily would look as she lazed in the depths of a perfumed bubble bath, the heavy curtain of that silver-blond hair no doubt secured on top of her head, and revealing the long, slender column of her bared throat and silky shoulders, the firmness of her breasts swelling tantalisingly above the bubbles—

'Oh, for goodness' sake!' Lily lost all patience with Dmitri's delay in leaving, knowing that if he didn't leave soon—*very* soon!—she was going to humiliate herself completely by bursting into tears in front of him. And she didn't intend giving him that satisfaction. 'Just close the door behind you on your way out!' She hurriedly crossed the room to step into that decadently opulent bathroom, before slamming and then locking the door securely behind her.

Only to lean weakly back against it as the tears began to fall hotly down her cheeks…

CHAPTER FIVE

'COULD I have my mobile phone back now?'

Dmitri raised dark brows as he turned from attending to a pan on the cooker hob and saw Lily standing in the kitchen doorway, obviously now completely refreshed after her journey. Her eyes were a clear bright blue, she'd slicked a pale lip gloss on those pouting lips and her beautiful, silky platinum-coloured hair fell straight and heavy over her shoulders and down the slenderness of her back. She was wearing a thin black sweater with tailored black trousers that fitted the smooth curves of her hips and bottom as though they'd been specially made for her.

Lily's cheeks became slightly flushed under the hooded intensity of Dmitri's gaze. 'I believe you took my mobile with you when you left my bedroom earlier, and I'd now like it back,' she repeated.

He gave a lazily unconcerned smile as he reached into the breast pocket of his casual white shirt and pulled out the slender black-and-chrome mobile before handing it to her. 'Don't worry, you haven't missed any calls or text messages.'

'I wasn't worried.' Lily dropped the phone back inside her shoulder bag.

'No?'

'No!' she reiterated, not knowing whether that was the truth or not. She *was* worried about Felix, obviously, and longed to speak to him—either on the phone or in person—but at the same time she didn't relish the thought of Dmitri being able to intercede in such a call.

She had enjoyed soaking herself in a scented bath for an hour or so earlier, finally relaxing as she'd got out to wrap a towel about herself before wandering barefoot through to the bedroom. Which was when she had realised that she couldn't find her mobile phone amongst the other things that had fallen out of her bag earlier onto the bed. A search amongst the slightly ruffled bedclothes, and then under the bed itself, had shown it wasn't there. Leading Lily to only one conclusion: Dmitri had to have taken the mobile with him when he'd left the bedroom!

The fact that he had just calmly handed it back to her, without so much as an apology for taking it in the first place, didn't improve her temper in the slightest. Which was probably as well, now that she once again found herself alone in the disturbing Dmitri Scarletti's company...

The kitchen wasn't at all what Lily had been expecting when she had followed the aroma of cooking food. It was far less opulent and more homely than the rest of the *palazzo*, with dried herbs hanging from the thick wooden beams in the ceiling amongst an array of copper pots and pans, and mellowed oak cabinets scarred with age. The large table and chairs standing on worn flagstones in the middle of the room looked equally as well-used.

But most disturbing of all was the man in front of her. Dmitri appeared completely relaxed as he stood in front of the old-fashioned range, stirring the reason for those delicious smells, with an open bottle of red wine on the worktop beside him, along with a half-full glass of the ruby liquid, showing that he had been enjoying taking sips of wine as he cooked.

He was dressed far less formally now, in a loose white shirt unbuttoned at the throat and with the sleeves turned up almost to his elbows, and a pair of faded jeans that fitted low on his lean waist and clung lovingly to his muscled thighs. The darkness of his hair was still damp from the shower he had obviously taken. He somehow looked younger, even sexier, and far less intimidating than he had earlier.

Damn it!

Lily had spent the past half an hour, as she'd dried her hair and then dressed, building herself up to a quiet fury—but one look at this relaxed, smiling Dmitri and she was once again aware of everything about him. The way his hair fell silkily onto his brow. The fact that there was no longer any shadow darkening that square and determined chin—evidence that he must have shaved. The unbuttoned shirt allowed her to see the start of the dark curling hair that no doubt covered most of his chest before dipping down below the waistband of his—

'Would you care for some red wine?'

Lily gave a startled blink as she realised she had been staring so intently at the utterly gorgeous man in front of her that she had completely forgotten he was probably using that time to stare right back at her—thereby allowing him to see how her cheeks had become flushed, her lips moist and slightly parted, even as her gaze hungrily devoured everything about him.

Double damn it!

This man held the key to her gilded cage, and as

such was *not* a man she should be drooling over, she told herself firmly.

Lily closed her eyes briefly before opening them again. 'Thank you,' she accepted huskily as she stepped farther into the kitchen. 'The food smells good,' she excused herself uncomfortably when her stomach gave an audible growl as a reminder that she hadn't eaten anything since those snacks on the plane.

'Let's hope that it tastes good too.' Dmitri took a second glass from the cupboard and poured some wine from the open bottle, handing it to her before topping up his own glass.

Lily took a welcome sip of the red wine, not in the least surprised at its delicious smoothness. She doubted a man as rich as Dmitri was reputed to be would ever have anything but the best wines in his cellar, and the finer the wine the smoother on the palate.

'Am I allowed to ask whereabouts in Rome we are?' Lily frowned, having become totally disorientated earlier, during her drive through the city.

'Of course.' He nodded, leaning back against one of the kitchen units, heavy lids lowered over piercing green eyes as he slowly sipped his own wine.

'Well?' she prompted impatiently, when he added nothing further.

He shrugged broad shoulders. 'You have not asked yet.'

Lily drew in an impatient breath. 'I'm asking now,' she grated between gritted teeth.

'We are in the area of Parioli. It's—'

'I know where it is.' She also knew what it was—the most prestigious and exclusive residential area in Rome! But then, where else would he live?

Lily had bought several books on Rome once her

ticket was booked, and had enjoyed poring over all the different areas and historical attractions of Rome in order to decide which places she wanted to visit while she was there. The area containing most of the homes of the wealthy and privileged inhabitants of Rome hadn't been one of them.

Dmitri eyed her from beneath dark lashes. 'You don't sound as if you approve.'

'It's not for me to approve or disapprove. It is what it is.' She gave a dismissive lift of her shoulders and avoided meeting his perceptive gaze. 'What are we having for dinner?' she asked as she looked down into the simmering cooking pots rather than at him.

'Spaghetti *alla carbonara*. It's—'

'I know what it is, Dmitri. We're quite cosmopolitan in England nowadays, you know,' she added snippily. 'We even eat with knives and forks on special days and holidays!'

Dmitri had been hoping that they might be able to spend a relaxing evening together—maybe enjoy some light conversation as they ate the meal he had cooked, and in the process dispel some of her antagonism towards him. Yet, after only a few minutes spent in her company, he knew she was spoiling for another fight rather than relaxed conversation!

Admittedly he should not have taken her mobile phone earlier, without first telling her what he was doing. Except by the time he had seen it lying on the bed, amongst her purse, a lipstick and a couple of paperback books, she had already locked herself in the bathroom, with the sound of running bathwater precluding any further conversation.

He sighed his impatience with her continued hostility. 'I remember eating in some very acceptable Italian restaurants during the years I lived in England.'

'I trust you passed that on to the proprietors? What a coup—to have a personal recommendation from Count Dmitri Scarletti!'

Yes, Dmitri acknowledged wearily, this promised to be a very long evening indeed. 'I was not Count Scarletti at the time, Lily,' he informed her quietly. 'My father did not die until the summer after I had left Oxford.'

Well, that had completely knocked the wind from her sails, she acknowledged a little guiltily, as she saw the pain he still felt at his father's death reflected in the grimness of his expression.

She winced. 'I'm sorry...'

'You are?' He looked surprised. 'I would have thought you might enjoy my obvious discomfort at the loss.'

'Really?' Lily bristled. Being angry with Dmitri on a personal level was one thing, but using the pain of his father's death as a means of hitting back at him would hardly have been fair. Admittedly this situation was decidedly odd, but she had never been a vindictive person—nor was she about to become one now. 'My own parents died in a car accident when Felix and I were only eighteen, so I'm hardly likely to relish hearing of someone else having suffered the same loss at an early age.'

'Even me?' Dmitri finished dryly.

'Even you,' Lily muttered. 'You must have been quite young when your father died,' she realised with a frown.

He nodded. 'My mother died when I was fifteen and my father when I was twenty-one.'

Lily thought of what she'd been doing when she was twenty-one. She had already worked her way through her degree course and had been preparing to embark on a student teacher course. It had been tough going, admittedly, but she'd only had herself to think about—bar the odd occasion when she'd had to bail her irresponsible brother out of trouble! But those things were nothing in comparison with the responsibilities Dmitri must have taken on at that tender age.

Oh, for goodness' sake, Lily, she instantly admonished herself. He's a multi-multi-millionaire—how tough could it have been?

Tough, she conceded ruefully. Money might have helped to cushion the situation for him, but Dmitri would still have been responsible for his much younger sister, and for all of the people who worked and lived under the Scarletti umbrella—either in the numerous companies he owned or on the family estates.

Oh, great—now she was starting to feel admiration for the man!

'Can we eat now?' she asked brusquely. 'I'm starving.'

Conversation over, Dmitri acknowledged ruefully. The subject of the conversation hadn't been exactly pleasant, but at least it had been conversation of a sort. 'Would you prefer to eat in here or upstairs in the formal dining room?'

A crease appeared on her creamy brow. 'Would that be the room I passed at the end of the hallway, just before the stairs down here?'

'Yes.'

Her nose wrinkled. 'Then I'd rather eat here—if that's okay with you.'

'Perfectly okay.' Dmitri turned back to the stove to

tip savoury pasta into a warmed serving bowl. 'And, if you would not consider it cooking, perhaps you would you care to get the garlic bread out of the warming oven?' he suggested with a teasing smile as he carried the steaming bowl of spaghetti to the table.

'I think I can do that, yes,' she came back pertly.

Dmitri turned back from the table in time to see Lily pick up an oven cloth before bending down to open the lower oven, so giving him a perfect view of her shapely bottom. Something guaranteed to turn his thoughts from food to another appetite entirely!

She really did have the most delectable bottom. Firm, with just enough roundness that a man would enjoy curling a hand about as he—

'More wine?' Dmitri prompted gruffly, and he moved to collect the bottle from the worktop, his expression strained as he took the spoons and forks from the drawer beside the oven.

'Er—yes. Thanks.' Lily straightened slowly, biting her lip as she carried the bowl of garlic bread over to the table, obviously slightly confused at the sudden change in his tone. 'Are you sure you don't mind eating down here?' She hesitated about sitting down on the chair Dmitri had pulled back for her.

No—in light of his previous thoughts about her bottom he wasn't at all sure about continuing to remain in the informal intimacy of the kitchen! His only concern at the moment should be ensuring Claudia's safe return. Certainly not imagining how he would enjoy clasping Lily's bottom as he took her on the dining table!

'Very sure,' he clipped, pushing her chair in as she finally sat down, then moving around the table to occupy the chair opposite as he felt himself drawn to the now-familiar apple-and-cinnamon scents of her hair.

Only to look up and find himself the focus her huge and puzzled blue eyes…

Beautiful eyes, Dmitri conceded. In fact, she was beautiful all over—from her silver-blond hair to the creamy smoothness of her pale skin. And as for the sensual allure of the pouting fullness of her lips—

Again, that was quite enough of that, he cautioned himself determinedly. Being kept here against her will as she was, Lily had absolutely no reason to like or trust him without him adding another layer to that distrust by allowing his increasing physical awareness of her to become an issue.

'Eat,' he instructed tersely, and he placed a large serving of pasta into her bowl before serving himself.

Lily raised mocking brows. 'Does that tone of voice usually work for you?'

Dmitri closed his eyes briefly in self-disgust, before looking across the table at her. 'I apologise. Circumstances are such that I am not…my usual self today.'

'And is your usual self better or worse than the self you are today?' she asked curiously.

'I would hope that he is at least more polite than I was just now,' he admitted ruefully.

'In that case, perhaps you would like to try again?' she suggested sweetly.

Dmitri relaxed back in his chair. 'Please eat before the food gets cold, Lily.'

'Much better,' she said with approval, and she picked up her fork to twine some of the spaghetti onto its tines before twirling it round. Only to have it fall off again before she could get it to her mouth. 'Damn,' she muttered, and tried again.

He chuckled softly. 'You do it like this.' He sat forward to pick up his fork and his spoon to demonstrate how the spoon should be placed on the end of the tines of the fork to keep the pasta in place.

'See?' He popped the pasta into his mouth.

Lily saw just fine—in fact, her gaze had been transfixed on his sensually wicked mouth the whole time. She just wasn't having any success in doing it herself, and forkful after forkful of the slippery pasta fell back into the bowl before making it as far as her mouth. But she was not about to give in and simply chop the spaghetti up and use her spoon to eat it, as she had so often seen other English people do.

'I could just starve to death with my current success rate!' she muttered, as yet another forkful of pasta fell back into the bowl. 'Maybe I should stick to the garlic bread!' She picked up a slice and took a healthy bite.

'Here—let me show you how.' He was still chuckling as he stood up to come round to her side of the table and bend over beside her, taking the spoon and fork from her unresisting fingers.

Mistake, Lily realised, tensing as every nerve ending in her body suddenly went on alert at his close proximity. Nor did it help that he looked so much younger, so much more approachable and so much more attractive, when he laughed. Almost boyishly handsome, in fact. Except there was absolutely nothing in the least boyish about Dmitri Scarletti!

A fact she was only too aware of now, as he stood far too close to her, the warm line of his arm brushing lightly against her shoulder, the loose white shirt falling forward and allowing her to see clearly the firm muscles of his chest and stomach, and the dark hair that lightly covered the whole of his chest before disappearing in a tantalising vee beneath the waistband of his jeans.

He smelled really good too—of spicy aftershave and hot, earthy male.

Oh, good Lord!

'Open your mouth, Lily,' he encouraged.

She raised startled lids. And then wished she hadn't as she realised his face was on a level with her own as he bent down beside her. Those pale green eyes were darkening to emerald as she looked at him, his breath a warm caress as she ran her tongue nervously across her slightly parted lips.

Her mesmerised gaze was transfixed on Dmitri's lips as he huskily repeated his earlier request. 'Open your mouth.'

Lily couldn't drag her gaze away from his as her lips slowly parted—only to have all the tastebuds in her mouth explode in pleasure as he neatly placed a forkful of the pasta *carbonara* onto her tongue.

'Oh, my God!' she breathed shakily once she was able to talk at all. 'That is *so* good!' She opened her eyes to look up at him appreciatively. 'You should open your own restaurant—no, of course you couldn't do that.' Lily grimaced as she immediately realised how ridiculous it was even to suggest that Count Scarletti become the chef of his own restaurant.

Dmitri had been held completely transfixed by the expression of pure ecstasy on her face as she ate the forkful of pasta, his shaft hardening as he was instantly bombarded by thoughts of how she would look exactly that same way in the throes of physical pleasure. Eyes closed. Throat arched. A dreamy smile upon her lips as she became completely lost to that ecstasy…

His gaze was still riveted on those slightly parted

lips as she breathed softly, and his own breath caught in his throat as the pink moistness of her tongue flicked out to lick a tiny smear of the *carbonara* sauce from her bottom lip.

Dmitri groaned softly in his throat as the throb of his shaft became almost painful as it grew harder, more swollen, with each rapid beat of his heart. As he imagined his own tongue flicking across the pouting sensuality of Lily's mouth. Licking. Tasting.

'I think I can manage on my own now, thank you, Dmitri.'

Lily's voice shattered those disturbingly sensuous images. He placed the fork and spoon down in her bowl and moved quickly round to the other side of the table, resuming his own seat. Before Lily could become aware of the throbbing evidence of his very obvious arousal.

This had never happened to him before, Dmitri realised with a frown. This sudden and complete awareness of a woman. And not just *any* woman, but one specific woman.

Oh, his relationships had been numerous over the years—brief, businesslike arrangements for the main part, that satisfied the woman's physical requirements as well as his own, while at the same time demanding nothing from him except the occasional expensive bauble as an added sign of his interest.

Dmitri had only known Lily a matter of hours, but he already knew her well enough to realise she was the type of woman who would throw any expensive bauble in a man's face if it was given to her under such circumstances!

Add into that equation the fact that he was keeping her here against her will—a prisoner in a gilded cage, as she put it so eloquently—and his sudden desire to kiss her, to caress and pleasure her, was the very madness she had accused him of earlier!

'Dmitri?'

'Yes?' He scowled darkly as he looked across the table at her from between narrowed lids.

Lily sat back slightly and eyed him warily, not altogether sure what to make of yet another sudden change in his mood. One moment he had been teasing her, the next seeming as if he might actually kiss her and then he had retreated so suddenly it was as if she carried some sort of contagious disease.

Which was perhaps how he thought of her, believing as he did that her brother was nothing but a fortune-hunter.

And of *course* the attractive, the rich, the titled Count Dmitri Scarletti hadn't been about to kiss her! What on earth was she thinking of? He'd only been being kind when he'd offered to teach her how to eat the pasta properly. The rest of it was purely in her own imagination. She would be wise to put such thoughts completely from her mind when she was the very last woman he would ever allow himself to be attracted to.

As Lily was attracted to him?

It would be useless even to try to fool herself into thinking otherwise. How could she possibly attempt to deny the attraction when she was so totally aware of every single thing about the man?

In fact, she was dangerously close to being infatuated with everything about him—the way he looked, the way he talked, the graceful way he moved, even the way he smelt. She physically ached with the effort of trying to resist her feelings.

Oh, hell…

CHAPTER SIX

THANKFULLY, by the time they had eaten the pasta and garlic bread, and loaded the bowls into the dishwasher, Lily had her wandering imagination back under control. It had been helped along by being able to relax as Dmitri related some of the more amusing stories of his time as a student in England. Designed, no doubt, to put Lily at ease.

It also didn't hurt that along the way they'd managed to empty one bottle of red wine and open another.

In fact, Lily was now so relaxed that she had almost forgotten her reasons for being here with him by the time they sat back down at the table to eat a selection of cheeses and sliced fruit.

'So, what made you decide to take up kick-boxing?' Dmitri prompted curiously.

Lily shot him a wry look. 'The fact that I'm five-foot-two-inches tall and weigh a puny seven-and-a-half stone.'

'I see.' He smiled. 'And no doubt such a skill would also be useful if you were ever to find yourself the reluctant guest of an Italian count!'

Lily met his gaze steadily. 'I didn't have quite this situation in mind at the time, but yes, no doubt it would.

Kick-boxing isn't about size or weight but ability.' She shrugged.

Dmitri frowned. 'I trust you know that I meant it earlier when I said I do not have any intention of harming you in any way? My quarrel is not with you but with your brother.' His expression hardened.

'And I trust you know that I meant it when I said I'm not worried?' she insisted.

'Yes.' He laughed. 'Obviously you are a young lady well accustomed to taking care of yourself.'

Lily frowned, sensing an implied criticism of her brother in his comment. 'What's that supposed to mean?'

'Exactly as it sounded.' Dmitri gave another shrug of those incredibly wide, muscular, biteable—

Okay, so maybe she had drunk a little too much of that deliciously smooth wine with her meal—because she had definitely started drooling again!

'As you're well aware, we do things differently in England, Dmitri.' She shook her head. 'I'm twenty-six years old, and I certainly don't need a man—especially my little brother—to take care of me, thank you very much.' She winced as she realised exactly what she had just said. 'Not that I'm faulting you for being protective of Claudia. Not at all. The situation is completely different, and obviously you've been responsible for her for a long time—' She broke off as he began to laugh. 'Am I overdoing the apology?'

'Just a little.' He smiled across at her—a smile that made her stomach turn somersaults.

Oh, good Lord...! It really was time she made her excuses and went upstairs to bed.

'It occurs to me that we have not had any dessert with our meal,' Dmitri said.

Lily looked surprised. 'Cheese and fruit don't count?'

'Not when the best ice cream in the world is available a short walk away, *cara*,' he replied.

Lily felt warmth enter her cheeks as she recognised that casual endearment—*cara* was the Italian equivalent of the English 'dear', wasn't it? Perhaps she wasn't the only one who had imbibed a little too much of that delicious red wine?

Was her imagination playing tricks on her, or had Dmitri just said the best ice cream in the world was a short walk away? Why would he have said that if she was supposed to be his prisoner? 'Are you suggesting that we go outside for a walk?'

Dmitri winced slightly. 'You really do consider yourself a prisoner here, don't you?'

'Maybe that's because I am?' Lily said bluntly.

'I had not—' Dmitri stopped, and then took a deep breath. 'Perhaps I was a little heavy-handed with you earlier.'

'Perhaps?' she said incredulously.

Dmitri continued to look across at her for several long minutes, appreciative of the things she had revealed about herself as they'd chatted over dinner—things that she was not perhaps even aware of. Such as the fact that she had obviously taken her role as the eldest of the twins very seriously since the death of her parents. That she had not taken a holiday in several years, and even then it had been in England. That she missed her brother very much. And, most importantly of all, perhaps, that this holiday in Italy was unexpected and something she could ill afford on a teacher's salary.

She had been looking forward to it with excited anticipation. Only to arrive in Rome and find herself then incarcerated without having seen her brother or a single one of the historic attractions she had obviously so looked forward to exploring.

Because Dmitri had decreed it should be so. Because, out of concern for his sister and anger towards Felix, he had decided to punish the only person who was available to him.

'There is no question of it. I was unreasonable with you on your arrival in Rome,' he acknowledged heavily.

Lily's eyes widened. 'Are you sure this isn't just the wine talking?'

Those sculptured lips curved into a teasing smile. 'Wine is like mother's milk to an Italian, Lily.'

'Really?' His lips on a woman's breast was an image that did absolutely nothing for Lily's earlier resolve to stop her imagination running away with her—and not just any woman's breast, either, but her own.

Okay, it was definitely time she excused herself and went to bed!

Past time, if her fantasies about this man were going to become so explicit she had actually felt a sharp spike of arousal—from the tingling of her breasts to the rapidly increasing dampness between her thighs...

'Where would you like to go?' Dmitri asked.

Bed probably wasn't the answer she should give right now! 'In all the guidebooks I read it said that the Trevi Fountain is particularly spectacular at night.'

'It is,' he confirmed, rising to his feet and coming around the table with the obvious intention of pulling her chair back for her. 'And, luckily for us, the best ice cream in Rome is just around the corner from it.'

She looked up at him uncertainly. 'At this time of night?'

'Of course. Roma is a city that never sleeps, Lily.'

'Like New York?'

Dmitri shook his head. 'In my experience New York is frenetic and Roma is romantic,' he corrected.

Oh, yes—a romantic walk in the moonlight with this devastatingly handsome man was *just* what she needed when her defences already felt like mush!

'Why have you suddenly become so…accommodating, Dmitri?' she asked awkwardly.

Those pale green eyes darkened with what looked like regret. 'Perhaps because I now realise exactly how…*un*accommodating I have been up till now?'

Lily stood up slowly, not sure that she altogether trusted Dmitri in this relaxed and charming mood. Definitely not sure she trusted herself in his company when he was in this almost playful mood!

Much as she welcomed the possibility of leaving the *palazzo*, if only for a short time, this collapse of her defences surely made it a recipe for disaster? Moonlight. Delicious ice cream. The Trevi Fountain. Dmitri Scarletti. Most especially the latter…

She turned, with the intention of telling him that it had been a long day and she thought it better if she went to bed now, only to tense as she realised how close he was now standing. He made no effort to step away from the back of her chair. So close Lily could once again feel the heat emanating from his body. Smell the aftershave that mingled so appealingly with hot, virile male. And see the dark shadow of stubble once more on his chin.

She could actually see the way the iris of his eyes had once again darkened to emerald as his gaze became fixed, apparently captivated by her slightly parted lips…

She couldn't breathe, and was pretty sure she couldn't have moved even if someone had shouted *Fire!* In fact, she felt unable to break away from his compelling gaze, her body actually starting to tremble as Dmitri continued to look deeply into her eyes.

Her throat moved convulsively as she swallowed. 'It's pretty late, Dmitri—' Lily didn't get any further in excusing herself as his arm moved firmly about her waist and he pulled her in close against him.

'You're right, Lily.' His voice was a low, husky growl. 'I am afraid it is far too late.'

His head moved down slowly and he captured her mouth with his own.

Lily heard herself groan low in her throat as his skilful lips opened hers, sipping, tasting, his tongue hot and demanding, while his arms tightened about her, crushing her breasts against the hard muscles of his chest. His hands moved down the slope of her back to cup her bottom and pull her in hard against him, and her legs began to tremble as she felt the pulsing evidence of his arousal against the softness of her stomach.

Her fingers dug into his broad shoulders as his mouth moved to trace the long column of her throat, his lips hot against her skin as she arched her neck to allow him freer access. Her legs felt so shaky now she was afraid that if she didn't cling on to him she might actually collapse at his feet.

She was being bombarded with sensations. Her senses were assaulted by his heat and overpowering strength, and at the same time she wanted to push even the thin barrier of his shirt out of her way, so that she could touch the skin beneath. Not just touch. But caress. Kiss. Taste. God, how badly she wanted to taste him—all of him.

What was Dmitri doing to her? How was he doing it to her?

She didn't behave like this. Had never felt like this with any of the men she had dated over the past ten years. She'd never wanted to rip anyone's clothes off before throwing off her own clothes and begging him to take her. Right here. On the table. Amongst the debris of their meal.

Dmitri could be her dessert! Lily instinctively knew he would taste rich and creamy and totally decadent. Sinful, in fact...

Not giving herself time to think, to regret, she unfastened the buttons on his shirt, her breathing ragged, fevered as she pulled it apart and gazed hungrily at his bared muscled chest before touching him tentatively, her fingers a light caress. He gave a low groan as she explored, touching him where he was most sensitive, holding his fevered gaze with her own as she ran the soft pad of her thumb experimentally across his skin and saw for herself the effect it had on Dmitri. His eyes glittered, and there was a slight flush now to those sculptured cheekbones.

'Lily...?' Dmitri hadn't planned on kissing her, let alone having her touch him like this.

He had been totally aware of her throughout their meal. Her smile. Her wistfulness. Her occasional sadness. A sadness he had longed to dispel. He had felt himself unwillingly drawn to her. To her beauty. Her heat. The musk of her arousal beneath the soft floral of the perfume she wore. And now that he had tasted the fullness of her lips, he wanted more...

'I am not sure I can stop this, *cara*,' he warned her gently, even as he rubbed the throb of his arousal against her yielding softness.

She seemed not to hear him as she lowered her head and placed her lips against his skin, her tongue feeling like the rasp of a cat's against his sensitised flesh, sending shockwaves of pleasure straight to the pulsing hardness of his shaft.

Dmitri buried his face in her throat as he surged hard and demanding against her, his hands tightly gripping her bottom now.

It was a perfect fit in his hands, just as he had imagined it would be, and he lifted her up until he felt himself nestled against the heat between her legs. He heard her soft groan as he began to move against her most sensitive part.

Dmitri cursed the layers of material that separated them, knowing that if they weren't there he would not be able to stop himself from burying himself inside her, as deep as he could go, and that once he had entered her heat he really would lose all control.

He lifted Lily to sit on the tabletop and his hands moved to the bottom of her sweater. He slowly lifted the woollen garment and his gaze became riveted on the fullness of her breasts, cupped in black lace, the nipples hard and deeply rose against that wispy material.

He wanted to taste them—*needed* to taste them—to take those rosy buds into his mouth and—

Too impatient to waste time locating the fastening of her bra, Dmitri simply pulled the lace down until the nipples popped over the top of those silky cups, full and hard and surrounded by darkly flushed areolae.

Lily gasped as he stepped in between her parted legs, his arousal a pulsing caress against her even through their clothes, his hair a silky brush against her skin as he lowered his head to her breast. Her initial gasp turned to a whimper, and her fingers dug into his shoulders as his lips fastened onto her nipple and he began to suck. Softly at first, and then harder, drawing her hungrily into his mouth. Her fingers became entangled in the thick darkness of his hair as she held him to her, lost in the pleasure that coursed through her body.

There was a soft sound as his lips released her breast. One of his hands was now cupping her there, clever fingers capturing the swollen nipple before pulling gently, rhythmically, as he turned the attention of his mouth to her other breast. The soft rasp of his tongue across the nipple, and the caress of his fingers against its twin caused a trembling through her body that seemed to begin at her toes and fingers and slowly work its way upwards and inwards, until it became centralised in a low, demanding throb between her thighs. Wave after wave of heated pleasure was building, ever building, until Lily felt as if she might shatter into a million pieces.

'Touch me, Lily!' Dmitri released her nipple to groan, the heat of his breath a tantalising caress against the dampness of her flesh. '*Dio mio*, Lily, I need your hands on me...' he entreated, as he took one of her hands and placed it on his jeans, over the hardness of him.

Lily felt it surge, pulse, as her palm pressed against him in a slow and rhythmic caress. Her own pleasure spiralled out of control as she looked down and watched as he once again drew her nipple into his mouth, his teeth grazing sensually against that sensitive bud.

Just as she had imagined there was something erotic, almost primitive, in seeing his much swarthier complexion against the paleness of her skin, his lashes a dark shadow against the flush of his cheeks, his tousled hair falling across his brow.

'What the—?'

Lily gave a protesting groan as Dmitri froze against her breast, taking several seconds to realise why. And then Lily heard it too. Mozart. Faint. But recognisably Mozart.

The ringtone she had chosen for her mobile!

It was like a having a bucket of ice cold water thrown over her. Over both of them.

Dmitri's arms fell back to his sides and he stepped back, a dark scowl on his brow as he looked down at her with hot green eyes.

Lily suddenly became uncomfortably aware of how wanton she must look, with her legs parted to accommodate him standing between her thighs, her black sweater pushed up and her breasts bared and swollen as they spilled over the cups of her bra.

Oh, help!

Dmitri watched from between hooded lids as Lily moved hastily off the table to turn away from him and straighten her clothing. Then she quickly searched inside her shoulder bag for the ringing mobile, the heavy curtain of her silver-blond hair falling forward to hide her flushed face, still slightly tangled from the caress of Dmitri's fingers.

What had just happened?

Why had it happened?

Admittedly she was a stunningly beautiful woman, but she was also Felix Barton's sister—the one woman in the world Dmitri should not have made love to!

He looked down at his own unbuttoned shirt, at once assailed with the memory of how Lily had pulled those buttons apart, how her bold lips had felt against his flesh. How her hands had—

'Hello?'

Dmitri's head came up like a predator that had just

scented prey as Lily finally found her mobile and took the call. Felix! It had to be him. Who else would telephone her at this time of night?

'Hey!' Lily protested as the phone was plucked out of her fingers before Dmitri placed it against his own ear. 'Dmitri!'

'Is that you, Barton?' He raised his other hand with the obvious intention of silencing her as he listened briefly before speaking again. 'Who is this?' he demanded harshly.

'Obviously not Felix,' Lily snapped as she retrieved her mobile. 'Yes. Sorry about that, Danny.' She shot Dmitri a resentful glance. 'Oh, just a…a friend of my brother's. No, he doesn't sound very friendly, does he?' She gave a forced laugh and Dmitri glowered across at her as he slowly refastened his shirt. 'Look, can I call you back tomorrow? Things are a little hectic here right now, and… Yes, of course I'll be sure and call you back,' she said lightly. 'Okay. Bye, Danny.'

A loaded silence filled the kitchen once she had ended the call and put the mobile back in her bag. She felt too stunned by what had just happened and the way her body still tingled in the aftermath of their passion to speak. She wasn't at all sure why *he* was suddenly silent.

It could be any number of things. Disappointment that the call hadn't been from Felix. Or maybe he was just disgusted by what had happened between them. Or perhaps it was a combination of the two; Lily certainly felt less than proud of her own wanton behaviour.

'Who is Danny?'

She gave Dmitri a startled look. 'Sorry?'

'Who is Danny?' he repeated through gritted teeth.

Or there could be a third reason for Dmitri's accusatory silence…

Not that Lily thought for a moment that he was in the least jealous that she had received a telephone call from another man. It was more likely that he was merely contemptuous of the fact that she had allowed him to make love to her when she obviously already had a man in her life. Except she didn't…

'Just a friend,' she dismissed.

Dmitri raised sceptical brows. 'And do your male *friends* usually telephone you at…' He glanced down at the plain gold watch on his wrist '…ten-thirty at night when you are away on your holidays?'

'Obviously the answer to that is yes—because one just did!' Lily said, giving an awkward shrug.

Dmitri studied her narrowly. 'One? How many male friends do you have?'

Lily felt the colour warm her cheeks at the derision in his tone. 'Dozens, actually,' she snapped.

'I see.' His delicious mouth thinned disapprovingly.

'Somehow I doubt that,' she scorned, knowing that each of them meant something entirely different by the term 'male friends'. But she had no intention of explaining herself to this man when he looked down at her so disdainfully!

He continued that look for several long seconds before turning away. 'If you will excuse me, I have some papers in my study I need to look through before tomorrow.'

'I'll just clear away in here, then, shall I?' she retorted, not in the least surprised that their romantic stroll in the moonlight now seemed to have been forgotten; apparently they didn't need the inducement of the moonlight to feel romantic. If that explosion of the senses could be called anything as tame as romantic...

Dmitri glanced at the table where they had just eaten dinner. And where he had just kissed Lily so passionately, so intimately...

One of the wine glasses—thankfully his own empty one—had toppled over onto the plate of cheese, and several pieces of fruit had spilled onto the table. The plates they had been using were in complete disarray.

Unbelievable!

Dmitri closed his eyes briefly to shut out the scene. Such behaviour, such loss of control, was totally out of character for him. His commitments and responsibilities did not allow for such impulsive, highly reckless behaviour. That he had behaved like that with the sister of a man he no longer trusted made his lapse doubly unacceptable to him.

He drew in a deep breath before answering. 'That would seem only fair, as I cooked the meal.' He quirked one dark brow in challenge.

There was no arguing with that, Lily acknowledged ruefully; Dmitri *had* prepared and cooked their delicious meal. So it was a pity that the pasta and garlic bread now seemed to have settled like a heavy weight in the bottom of her stomach. 'Fine,' she accepted curtly. 'I'll see you in the morning, then.'

He nodded. 'If you would care for a swim before breakfast there is a heated pool in the east wing of the *palazzo.*'

The *palazzo* had its own heated swimming pool?

Why was Lily surprised? The place was big enough to house an indoor football pitch if Dmitri had decided he wanted one! 'As it's December, I didn't bother to bring my bathing costume with me,' Lily admitted.

'I have no problem with you skinny dipping...'
Those pale green eyes swept over Lily from her head
to the tips of her toes, before settling back on her now
slightly flushed face.

'I have a problem with it!' Lily said firmly.

Dmitri shrugged as he walked towards the doorway
out into the hallway. 'The offer is there if you should
change your mind.'

'I won't,' she stated flatly. She had already behaved
in a reckless way with this man, she didn't need to ask
for trouble by swimming in the nude! More trouble,
that was...

Heaven only knew what Dmitri thought of her after
that wanton display—if it was anything like the things
Lily had been thinking about herself then it wasn't in
the least complimentary.

'Aren't you going to take my mobile with you this
time?' Lily couldn't resist calling after him—and then
wished she hadn't as she realised she had just reminded
him that her mobile was her only means of contacting
anyone outside the *palazzo*.

His shoulders tensed as he paused in the doorway
before turning slowly to look at her speculatively.
'Would you tell me if you were to receive a telephone
call or text from your brother?'

'Yes, of course I'd tell you.' Lily didn't even have to
think about her answer. She knew that beneath Dmitri's
arrogance he was genuinely worried about his sister;
it would be cruel of her not to tell him if she were to
hear from the eloping pair.

He nodded. 'Then you may keep the mobile.'

'How kind of you to allow me to!' Lily felt stung
into retaliating.

A brief but humourless smile curved his lips. 'I thought so, yes. Goodnight, Lily.'

'Night, Dmitri,' she mumbled in reply, waiting until she was sure he had definitely gone before sinking slowly down onto one of the kitchen chairs, her heated cheeks buried in her hands, as she was instantly bombarded with memories of every arousing moment of being in his arms…

Forty-eight.

Dmitri continued to count the number of lengths of the pool he had swum so far as he pushed away from the side and once again struck out powerfully for the opposite end.

Forty-nine.

Neither the exercise nor the refreshingly warm water had done anything to cool his ardour from an hour ago, when he had left Lily in the kitchen and, instead of going to his study as planned, decided to take up his own suggestion of going for a swim. Secure in the knowledge, of course, that Lily had no intention of taking up the offer; having her here too, with or without a bathing costume, would certainly negate his own reasons for being here!

Fifty.

Not that this deliberately punishing exercise had in the least helped him in the least to understand—or accept—his unprecedented response to Lily.

Fifty-one.

She was beautiful, yes. But Dmitri had known and bedded many beautiful woman in his thirty-six years. So what was it about her, specifically, that now made it as impossible to put the touch of the silky softness of her skin from his mind as it had been for him to resist kissing her in the kitchen earlier? *Dio mio*—in the kitchen, on top of the table where they had just eaten dinner, of all things!

Fifty-two.

And what was this man Danny to Lily? A friend, she had said. But what sort of friend? A friend who just happened to be male? Or was the other man more than that? Surely a man who was just a friend wouldn't have called her quite so late at night? And long distance, at that.

Fifty-three.

Yet why should it matter to him who or what this man Danny had been, or still was, in Lily's life? It did not, obviously. Except she had given him the impression she did not have a man currently in her life...

Fifty-four.

It should not matter to him one way or the other whether Lily had lied to him earlier. It did not matter to him! Why should it? Lily meant nothing to him. Except as the annoying sister of the man who had eloped with Dmitri's own sister.

Fifty-fi—

Dmitri stilled as the flashing of red lights caught and held his attention and he stared up at the security panel on the wall beside the door into the swimming complex. The lights only flashed like that when an intruder was trying to break into the *palazzo*.

Or when someone was trying to break out...

CHAPTER SEVEN

'WHAT did you think you were doing?' Dmitri growled, concentrating on wrapping a bandage about the cut on Lily's hand as she sat in front of him on one of the kitchen chairs.

She gave a pained wince. Not because of the discomfort from the cut to her hand, but because of the obvious disgust in Dmitri's tone as he asked her why she had broken a small window in the kitchen in an effort to try and get out of the *palazzo*.

Obviously with hindsight—and the arrival of four hefty employees of the security company who monitored the system installed in the *palazzo*, along with several local police officers—it hadn't been such a good idea, after all.

Lily had cleared away in the kitchen before going upstairs to her bedroom. Where she had instantly felt the sharp edge of her confinement. That, and also the full force of her embarrassment at her behaviour in the kitchen earlier. No—nothing so mild as embarrassment. She had been totally devastated as she was bombarded with memories of her own lack of inhibition.

She just didn't behave in that way. With any man. Let alone one who was keeping her a virtual prisoner— albeit a pampered one—in his home. And the thought of having to face him across the breakfast table in the morning had simply been too mortifying for her even to contemplate.

The obvious solution to her dilemma had seemed to be to remove herself from the *palazzo* and the temptation its dangerously attractive owner represented to her still shaky defences.

Great in theory—not so good in practice!

Oh, dragging a chair over and climbing up to break the small window above the sink in the kitchen hadn't proved too much of a problem. It had been easy, in fact. Too easy, Lily had realised belatedly...

She had never even seen a sophisticated security system like the one installed in the *palazzo* before. She'd had no idea, for instance, that instead of the loud ringing of alarm bells she might have expected when she broke the window—and at the time had been grateful not to hear—an alarm actually went off in the offices of the security company itself, which in turn then sent a call through to the local police.

Lily had barely had the chance to move the sharp remnants of glass from the shattered window out of her way, cutting her hand in the process, before she was pounced upon by half a dozen excessively muscled men—four from the security company and two policemen!

Trying to explain that she was trying to get out of the *palazzo* rather than into it had proved virtually impossible when none of the men spoke English and Lily spoke hardly any Italian. It had been left to Dmitri, wearing only a towel draped about his waist and with his hair wet and tousled, to explain the situation to the security company and the police. Although again, not speaking anything but rudimentary Italian, Lily wasn't quite sure what that explanation had entailed.

How on earth did any man go about explaining that a woman was trying to break out of his home and not into it? Especially when that man was only wearing a towel about his waist to cover his own nakedness!

And he was still only wearing a towel—a fact she was only too well aware of as he stood in front of her, bandaging her cut hand...

If she had thought she'd felt embarrassed earlier it was nothing to the humiliation she felt now. The police, and finally the men from the security company, after putting a temporary cover over the broken window, had gone, and she was once again left alone with Dmitri.

'Well?' he rasped impatiently as he secured the end of the bandage before stepping slightly away from her.

Allowing Lily to breathe again at last. Well...sort of. She was still aware of the fact that Dmitri had probably been taking a shower or something when the alarm went off; his hair was still slightly damp even now, and of course he only wore that towel draped about his waist. Leaving the broad expanse of his chest and his long muscled legs completely bare...

'Well, what?' She looked anywhere but directly at him.

Dmitri snorted, not knowing if he wanted to shake her or just walk away in disgust—before he did something much more disturbing to her.

He scowled down at her. 'Did it not occur to you that breaking a window would breach the security system?'

The stubborn jutting of her chin did nothing to alleviate her sudden impression of vulnerability; she looked about sixteen years old, dressed in faded jeans along with the black sweater she had worn earlier, and with her hair secured in a loose plait down her back. 'Of course it occurred to me—I just thought I would have time to get safely away before anyone responded. And I would have done too, if I hadn't been delayed by getting something to wrap around my hand,' she added, looking annoyed.

Dmitri gave a sigh of frustration as he turned away to run one of his own hands impatiently through his rapidly drying hair; he had paused only long enough earlier to pick up a towel before hurrying from the pool complex to the west wing. Probably as well—otherwise he might have needed to actually go to the police station in order to have her released from a prison cell. He'd wanted to get there quickly in case the outspoken Lily said or did something to cause the police to arrest her, anyway!

He shake his head. 'Safely away where? Lily, there is nowhere in Rome that I could not find you if I wished to do so,' he explained as she frowned up at him.

'Oh.' She looked nonplussed, but didn't question his claim—probably because his expression alone was enough to tell her that he meant what he said. 'Oh, come on, Dmitri.' She grimaced as he continued to frown. 'You can't blame a girl for trying!'

'Yes, I can—when I end up having to lie to the police!' Dmitri snarled.

Lily eyed him curiously. 'In what way did you lie to them?'

He scowled darkly. 'I told them we had had a lovers' spat—that I walked out of the kitchen and left you to it, after which you threw something at the window in a temper and broke it.'

Those sky-blue eyes widened. 'I don't have a temper!'

'Fortunately they did not know that.'

'And they actually believed you?'

'Probably not,' he accepted.

'I would say definitely not,' Lily scoffed. 'If we had argued, and I really had been angry enough to throw something, then I would have made sure it was at you—not a window!'

'I am well aware of that,' Dmitri rasped. 'Fortunately the police and the men from the security company were not, and wisely decided to accept my romanticised version of what took place.'

Which explained the reason for the knowing smiles and winks of the security men before they'd left. 'No doubt you all had a good laugh at the little lady's expense?' She stood up abruptly.

Dmitri skewered her with that piercing green gaze. 'I assure you that so far I have not found anything in the least amusing about this situation.'

'That makes two of us!' she retorted.

Dmitri wondered if anything could succeed in shaking this woman's independence of will.

Yes, of course it could. Obviously what had happened between them after dinner had disturbed her enough for her to try and break out of the *palazzo*.

Dmitri still flinched inwardly when he recalled entering the kitchen to see a vulnerable Lily surrounded by a threatening group of men, and with blood dripping down her hand and onto the tiled floor from where she had cut herself.

Because she had wanted to get away from him.

Because she had been so traumatised by the depth of the intimacies they had shared she did not wish to remain here and risk having them repeated.

Admittedly the circumstances of finding themselves

alone here together were unusual, and their lovemaking had been unwise to say the least, but Dmitri could never remember a woman being so desperate to escape his attentions that she had attempted to flee into the night as if pursued by the devil himself!

He looked at her closely. 'Are you so determined to leave here you would risk injury to yourself in an attempt to do so?'

Lily raised defensive brows. 'My intention was obviously to get away from here, not to injure myself.'

His nostrils flared. 'I am still not sure the cut on your hand does not require stitches—'

'I heal quickly,' Lily cut in firmly, putting the hand in question behind her back—hoping out of sight would prove to be out of mind. Although, knowing Dmitri, she somehow doubted it would achieve that objective! 'Can we just go to bed now? I mean—' She broke off with a self-conscious wince as the embarrassed colour warmed her cheeks. 'I'm going to bed,' she amended. 'Alone. You can do whatever you please.'

'To quote you from earlier, "How kind of you to allow me to,"' Dmitri came back dryly.

Her eyes flashed deeply blue. 'I'm tired, I have an aching hand, and I feel slightly embarrassed at having brought the police and security company here—'

'Only slightly?' he jeered.

'*Slightly* embarrassed,' Lily reiterated. 'And I am decidedly cranky. Do you really want to mess with me any more tonight?' She met his gaze challengingly.

If it hadn't been entirely inappropriate to the situation Dmitri knew that he would have been tempted to laugh at her manner of speech; she really didn't allow herself to feel cowed by anyone or anything. As her thwarted attempt to escape from him testified…

He sighed. 'Once the glazier has replaced the window tomorrow morning I will take you anywhere you wish to go.'

'You're suggesting we go out for ice cream and to see the Trevi Fountain?' Her heavy tone made it sound like some sort of bizarre punishment on Dmitri's part.

'No,' he said through gritted teeth. 'I meant I will drive you to a hotel.'

Her eyes widened. 'Really?'

Dmitri's irritation deepened at the disbelief in her tone. 'Really,' he echoed tersely.

Lily eyed him warily, not altogether sure she completely trusted this about face. 'What about Claudia and Felix?'

His expression darkened just at the mention of the missing couple. 'I will have to find some other way of locating them.'

'How exactly?'

'I have no idea as yet!' he said harshly. 'Only that I will endeavour to do so.'

Because Lily had created an awkward situation for him by trying to break her way out of here? Or because he genuinely felt regret about keeping her confined when she would obviously rather be somewhere else? Either way—

'Are you cold?' Lily frowned. She was sure she'd seen him give a slight shiver. Or perhaps it was just a shudder of revulsion at the memory of having his home invaded by the police in the middle of the night!

'Why on earth would I be cold?' he said scathingly. 'It is late December, one o'clock in the morning, my window has been broken and I am wearing only a towel. Why *should* I be cold?'

'There's no need to be sarcastic,' Lily said indignantly.

'There is every reason—' He broke off exasperatedly, breathing hard. 'Tell me, Lily, does this sort of thing happen to you in England?'

She gave a puzzled frown. 'What sort of thing?'

Dmitri raised dark brows. 'Being kidnapped by an Italian count. Made love to on a kitchen table.' After the discomfort he had suffered for the past hour he felt a certain grim satisfaction as he saw the colour warm Lily's cheeks. 'Housebreaking. Being questioned by the police.'

Her cheeks remained flushed. 'There aren't an awful lot of Italian counts in England. I was breaking out of the house not into it. And the police could hardly question me when I don't speak Italian and they don't speak English. So the answer to your question is no, Dmitri, nothing like this has ever happened to me in England!'

Dmitri noted that she had chosen not to offer even the suggestion of a contradiction over their lovemaking. Because that had happened to her in England? Or because she was embarrassed that it had happened at all?

'Please just go to bed, Lily,' he advised, a nerve pulsing in his tightly clenched jaw.

She shook her head. 'No—you go and put some clothes on and I'll make you a pot of hot coffee.' She moved to the coffee percolator on the worktop and filled it up with water, before going to the refrigerator to take out the ground coffee. 'Although why on earth you were taking a shower at almost one o'clock in the morning is beyond me.'

'I was not taking a shower,' Dmitri denied, frowning as she continued to make the coffee; he was used to people doing what he said when he said it—if not sooner!—something Lily either didn't appreciate or deliberately chose to ignore.

She turned after spooning the coffee into the filter and switching on the machine. 'Then what *were* you doing?'

Nor was Dmitri accustomed to people questioning his actions—something else that she felt absolutely no hesitation in doing. He found it extremely irritating, while at the same time strangely refreshing…

For fifteen years Dmitri had said and done exactly as he wished, without criticism or question from anyone. To find himself subjected to the curiosity of a woman who stood only as tall as his shoulder, weighed as little as a pubescent teenage girl—even if she was far from being one—and who had a tongue as sharp as a razor, was something of a shock. A little like living amongst sheep for years only to then find himself confronted by a lioness!

'Dmitri?'

He felt a brief warmth as she continued to call him by his first name. 'Yes?' he answered huskily.

She shot him a pointed look. 'I asked where you were when the security alarm went off.'

'In the pool.' *Cooling off.* An exercise in futility when he was heating up again rapidly now that he was once again back in her company.

'Oh.' She blinked. 'So you aren't completely naked under that towel?'

This time Dmitri couldn't stop the smile that curved his lips. 'Not completely, no.'

Not too much of a comfort when Lily was pretty sure Dmitri was the sort of man who would wear body-hugging swimming briefs. Possibly in black. The sort that defined more than they hid.

And why not? He certainly had the sort of lean and muscled body that would look—

No—not going there. How he did or didn't look in a pair of swimming briefs was of absolutely no interest to her.

Liar!

How he looked was of far more interest than was good for her!

She turned away from the mockery she could now see glinting in his eyes. 'Coffee's almost ready,' she announced brightly, after checking the pot.

'Is that my cue to go and put some clothes on?' he murmured softly.

It was certainly his cue to go somewhere! Anywhere. As long as it was well away from the confines of this kitchen. 'Unless you want to continue being cold, yes.' She affected an uninterested shrug—one that probably didn't succeed in convincing either of them of her sincerity.

No one man should be allowed to possess the sinful good looks that Dmitri did. That air of haughtiness that in no way disguised the animal magnetism beneath. The hard and muscled body that drew her attention like a moth to a flame.

'Lily?'

She drew in a deep breath even as she schooled her features into polite query before turning. 'Yes?'

'Just so that you know I was telling the truth just now...' He slowly removed the towel from about the leanness of his waist, revealing that he did indeed wear brief black swimming trunks that left absolutely nothing to the imagination. Lily's imagination, at least!

Had he deliberately removed the towel in an attempt to cause her further embarrassment? Or because he knew the effect his near-nakedness was already having on her?

If he hadn't known before then he did now, because she couldn't take her eyes off him. Her cheeks became flushed with her rapidly escalating arousal, her breasts were once again feeling full and tingling, and between her thighs she was starting to ache gently.

Dmitri's bare shoulders were so very wide and powerful. His muscled chest was covered in that fine dusting of dark hair that only hours ago Lily had caressed. His stomach was flat and lean—he might sit behind a desk in an office most of the time, but he must also work out regularly to achieve that washboard six-pack. As for that telling bulge beneath the thin black material of his bathing trunks...

Lily moved her gaze back almost desperately to the hard, sculptured beauty of his face, glaring at him as she saw the open amusement that he made no effort to hide. 'Very nice, Dmitri,' she bit out as she slowly, deliberately, looked him up and down from head to toe. 'Now, would you mind not being such an exhibitionist and putting some clothes on?'

This time he was unable to quell a laugh as Lily spoke to him and looked at him in that condescending way; she really was the most intriguing woman he had met for a very long time. If ever.

A sobering thought in itself... Becoming intrigued by the beautiful and outspoken Lily Barton was certainly not on Dmitri's future list of things to do. His immediate list, however, was a different matter altogether...

'Don't wait up for me if you would rather go up to bed,' he said as he squashed that tempting thought by glancing away on the pretext of rewrapping and securing the towel about his waist.

Her brows rose. 'I'd like to stay and have coffee too––unless you would rather I didn't?'

Dmitri's jaw tightened just at the thought of Lily still being there when he returned. Waiting for him... 'And what possible reason could I have for not wanting you to stay and enjoy a cup of coffee when you were actually the one to make it?'

'No reason.' She shrugged. 'You just seemed... Well, as if you would rather be alone.'

Dmitri was accustomed to being alone. Claudia still lived at the *palazzo* with him, yes, but she was a late riser and he was an early one, meaning that they rarely ate breakfast together. Claudia also invariably went out in the evenings—latterly with Felix, he now realised!—and Dmitri was usually out at his office for most of the day and early evening. Meaning that brother and sister lived fairly separate lives for the main part.

In fact, Dmitri did not remember the last time he had spent as much time all at once in the company of a person he was not related to or discussing business with.

Even his physical relationships were usually conducted with the least amount of socialising, and Dmitri had always made a point of never spending the whole night with any of those women. Mutual physical gratification was one thing—eating breakfast or spending the day with any of those women was not something he had ever felt the inclination to do.

So this prolonged time spent with Lily was unusual for him. Something he should perhaps have thought of before he'd had her brought here...

'If it takes you this long to answer then I was obviously right in my deduction,' Lily drawled ruefully.

'I'll just pour myself a cup of coffee and disappear upstairs with it before you come back—'

'It only took me so long because I considered the question too ridiculous to necessitate a reply at all,' Dmitri said.

'Ridiculous?' Lily repeated slowly, her gaze wary as she waited expectantly for another one of his now familiar set downs. Nor was she disappointed!

He shrugged bare shoulders. 'Ridiculous in that I see no relevance to me as to whether you choose to drink your coffee down here or upstairs in your bedroom.'

Ouch!

Lily deliberately stood her ground as she raised blond brows. 'Now who's getting cranky?'

She watched as Dmitri closed his eyes briefly, as if by doing so he might shut her out of his awareness altogether—or in the hope that she might just have disappeared by the time he opened them again.

No such luck! 'I'm still here, Dmitri,' she taunted gently.

Pale green eyes glittered as he raised his lids to glare across the room at her. 'So I see.' He breathed deeply. 'I will return for my coffee shortly.' He strode from the kitchen, amazingly still managing to look every inch—every delectable, edible inch—the proud and haughty Count Dmitri Scarletti, despite being barefoot and half naked.

Leaving Lily to make the choice as to whether she should go back upstairs or whether she should stay exactly where she was…

CHAPTER EIGHT

'So you decided to take your coffee upstairs with you last night, after all, then?' Dmitri folded his lean length down into the chair opposite Lily's at the kitchen table, where she sat at seven-thirty the following morning already eating toast and drinking coffee.

Instantly reminding her that she had taken the cowardly way out the previous evening and not waited for Dmitri to return from dressing...

At the time she had decided that caution was probably the better part of valour—which was a polite way of saying she simply hadn't trusted herself to spend any more time in his provocatively disturbing company last night.

She placed her coffee cup carefully down on the saucer, continuing to look down at that saucer as she answered him. 'I was tired after all the travelling and—and excitement of yesterday.'

'That is one way of putting it, I suppose,' Dmitri drawled.

Lily glowered as she looked at him properly for the first time this morning, her eyes widening slightly as she saw he was wearing faded blue jeans and a black cashmere sweater that emphasised the width and power of his shoulders. The sleeves of the sweater were pushed up to just below his elbows, revealing the strength of his arms and wrists—

Oh, good Lord—she couldn't be stupid enough to find even his arms and wrists sexy, could she?

She had expected him to be dressed in readiness for going to his office this morning, to continue his search for Claudia and Felix. Once he had seen Lily safely delivered to a hotel, of course. 'I was referring to the way the police descended on the *palazzo* last night.'

'No doubt a thrilling tale for you to tell your friends on your return to England,' Dmitri said dryly as he sat forward to pour himself a cup of coffee from the pot in the centre of the table.

Lily bristled. 'If you think I enjoyed even one moment of that—that embarrassing episode, then you are sadly mistaken! In fact, I would prefer never to think of it again.'

Dmitri remained completely unruffled by her vehemence, and he sipped his coffee before replying. 'Not even as an amusing tale to relate to your grandchildren one day?'

'Of the night I tried to break out—unsuccessfully, I might add—of an Italian count's *palazzo*?' She eyed him scathingly.

He bared his teeth in a smile. 'Exactly.'

Lily grimaced. 'I think I'll pass, thanks.' Especially when those grandchildren might then ask what she had been doing locked away in there in the first place! Not only did this situation reflect badly on Felix, but her own behaviour so far had been less than suitable for telling any future children or grandchildren she might have.

Dmitri knew he should not be enjoying Lily's obvious discomfort, but after the unsatisfactory night's sleep he'd had he was feeling less than indulgently inclined towards her this morning.

Coming back down the stairs last night and discovering she had taken him at his word and already gone up to bed had been the start of that dissatisfaction. He had then wondered—despite having made the offer to take her to a hotel in the morning—if she had indeed gone to bed or if she was up in her room even now, plotting and planning some other way of leaving the *palazzo*. Hopefully avoiding detection this time!

Consequently, by the time he'd gone up to his own bedroom he'd been feeling less than sleepy, and had remained awake for some time after that, watching the security panel in his bedroom in case the alarm should go off again. Even once he had fallen into an uneasy sleep he was sure he had still been half listening for the sound of someone moving stealthily through the building!

To come downstairs this morning and find her calmly seated at the kitchen table enjoying her breakfast—and looking completely rested into the bargain—only increased his feelings of irritation at his own lack of sleep. 'As you wish,' he said unsympathetically. 'The glazier should be here shortly, and in the meantime I have some telephone calls to make.'

'In connection with Felix and Claudia?' she prompted sharply.

His mouth tightened. 'As it happens, yes. I take it you have still not heard from your brother?'

'No.' If Lily was being honest she was starting to get more than a little annoyed with Felix herself now. Not only had her brother just disappeared, but he hadn't even bothered to so much as check whether or not Lily had received his message in time to cancel her trip to

Rome. None of which was helped by the fact that Lily had realised first thing this morning that today was Christmas Eve.

'The glazier should not take long to replace the window, and then I will be free to drive you to a hotel—if that is convenient for you?'

'Yes. Yes, of course it is.' Lily sat up straighter in her chair as he came straight to the point; obviously idle chit chat was not the order of the day. 'Obviously I don't have any other plans for today.'

'Obviously not,' he conceded dryly.

'But I could always get a taxi to a hotel rather than put you to any trouble on my behalf. Any more trouble on my behalf,' she corrected as Dmitri raised mocking brows.

His smile was strained. 'It is no trouble, I assure you.'

Lily gave him a small smile. 'No doubt you'll just be glad to see the back of me?'

'No doubt.'

Well, you asked for that one, Lily, she seethed inwardly. Gave him the perfect opening, in fact. 'Is there anything I can do to help you?'

Dmitri eyed her coolly. 'Such as?'

'Make some of the telephone calls for you? No, that isn't going to work when I don't speak Italian,' she acknowledged ruefully. 'There must be *something* I can do!'

His mouth twisted into another semblance of a smile. 'I cannot think of anything.'

Great. Now Lily felt completely superfluous. Which she obviously was.

Was it any surprise that he couldn't wait to get rid of her when, instead of being a means of contact with

Felix, as Dmitri had obviously hoped she would be, she had become nothing more than a liability. A liability who last night had caused him deep embarrassment with his security firm and the police. And she was another inconvenience to him this morning by making him wait at home for a glazier to replace the broken window. No wonder he couldn't wait to get rid of her!

But was Lily equally eager to leave?

That was an interesting question. And one that she hadn't been able to answer either last night, as she lay in the warmth and comfort of her four-poster bed, or this morning, when she'd come downstairs to make herself some breakfast in the now-familiar kitchen.

Admittedly she had initially been forced to stay here against her will, and Dmitri's agreeing to her leaving this morning was what she had been asking for ever since her arrival.

But once she left it was very unlikely that she would ever see him again.

Which was good—wasn't it?

That was what she was still trying to decide!

She stood up. 'I'll just clear away here and then go upstairs and pack my things.' She once again avoided looking at him as she carried her plate and cup over to the dishwasher.

Dmitri watched Lily as she walked across the kitchen. The blue of her fitted sweater was an exact match in colour for her eyes, and her hair was once again a loose curtain of platinum about her shoulders and down the length of her slender spine. Her black jeans fitted smoothly over the delectable curve of her bottom as she bent over the dishwasher.

Good sense told Dmitri that the sooner he was rid of such a distraction the happier he would be. The now familiar throbbing hardness of his arousal—this time just from his observation of the pertness of Lily's bottom as she bent over the dishwasher—obviously didn't agree with him.

Once again he was completely at a loss to understand why he reacted so intensely, so immediately to a schoolteacher from England, when he had escorted—bedded—some of the most beautiful and accomplished women in Italy. It was totally illogical.

He stood up as well. 'I will be in my study when the glazier arrives.' He turned away before she was able to see the evidence of his physical reaction to her, irritated that a certain part of his anatomy was wilfully glad to see and be with her!

Lily looked up in time to see Dmitri leaving the kitchen. There was a frown between her eyes as she slowly straightened. Obviously even being in the same room with her was a strain for him this morning.

'Does the glazier or the representative of the security company have need of me?'

'No, the glazier is still replacing the window.' Lily stood hesitantly in the doorway of Dmitri's study, not in the least encouraged by his slightly hostile greeting or the coldness of his expression as he sat behind the large mahogany desk that dominated the elegant wood-panelled room with its large picture window. 'I've finished my packing.' It had taken Lily all of ten minutes to replace the few things she had taken from her case the day before. 'And I wondered if you'd had any luck with your phone calls?'

'None whatsoever,' he admitted as he threw down onto the desktop the pen he had been making notes with. 'None of our friends or acquaintances have seen or heard from Claudia, and there is no record of Felix or Claudia taking a flight from Rome airport in the past twenty-four hours.'

'Oh.' Lily grimaced. 'What about the other airports in Italy?'

He frowned. 'Sorry?'

She shrugged as she leant against the doorframe. 'Well, it seems to me that Felix and Claudia are both intelligent enough to have realised you would concentrate your efforts on Rome airport. Especially as they conveniently left Claudia's car at a Leonardo da Vinci for you to find,' she added. 'So I wondered if there's another airport close by? One they could have taken a taxi to? Where they could then have taken a flight to another part of Italy, perhaps?'

Dmitri's expression was thoughtful as sat back in his leather chair. 'Perhaps I should have accepted your offer of help earlier...'

Her eyes widened. 'You should?'

'Two heads are obviously much better than one.' Waves of frustrated energy came off him as he sat forward to pick up the telephone before punching in the appropriate numbers. 'I should have thought of this earlier... Paolo?' His attention quickened as his call was obviously answered. *'Si.'* Dmitri launched into a stream of Italian that Lily didn't have a hope of understanding. *'Si, si, si. Grazie,* Paolo.' He slowly replaced the receiver to look dazedly across the room at Lily. 'Claudia and Felix chartered a plane and pilot and flew from a private airport to Milano yesterday morning.'

Which certainly explained why there had been no record of them flying out of Leonardo da Vinci airport! But *Milan?* Why on earth would they have flown to Milan? 'Does Claudia have friends or relatives there?'

'No.' Dmitri's mouth was tight. 'But my delay in realising what they had done will have given them a twenty-four hour window in which to arrange a flight out of Milano.'

'To where?'

'That is what I have yet to find out,' he bit out tautly.

Lily chewed on her bottom lip as she saw the grimness of Dmitri's expression as he made another phone call—her little brother was in deep, deep trouble! Probably the biggest trouble he had ever been in in his life. Once Dmitri caught up with him, Felix would be lucky if he was even allowed to remain in Italy— let alone see Claudia again.

And Lily was left standing there like a spare part, not knowing what to do with herself while Dmitri engaged in another rapid-fire conversation in Italian with whomever it was he had telephoned now.

Self-pity wasn't something that she had ever allowed herself to indulge in—mainly because she had been too busy these past eight years just managing to keep all the balls of her life in the air rather than letting them crash to the ground—but she was definitely starting to feel a little sorry for herself now. It was Christmas Eve, after all, and it looked as if Dmitri was almost ready to leave the *palazzo* to drive her to a hotel. Where she would no doubt spend the rest of the day alone. And tomorrow too. Really not the way in which Lily had envisaged spending her Christmas Day!

'Where are you going?' Dmitri placed his hand over the mouthpiece of the telephone in order to talk to Lily as he realised she had turned away, with the obvious intention of leaving him to the privacy of his telephone call.

She gave a small shrug as she looked at him over

her shoulder. 'I thought I would just take my suitcase downstairs so that I'm ready to leave whenever you are.'

So that she was ready to leave...

Dmitri had actually forgotten his offer to drive her to a hotel in these past few minutes, because he finally felt as if he was making progress where Claudia and Felix was concerned. But he remembered it now. It also occurred to him that Lily, once at the hotel, would then be completely alone over the Christmas holiday. Just as Dmitri would. Which had never been a problem for him before.

It was not a problem for him now, either, he told himself harshly. It was Lily of whom he was thinking—not himself. 'There is no rush, is there?' Did her expression brighten slightly? Dmitri wasn't sure.

'No,' she answered. 'No, of course there's no rush.' She smiled. 'I was just going to make some coffee for the men downstairs. Perhaps you would like a cup too?'

'I would—thank you,' Dmitri agreed warmly.

Too warmly? What on earth was the matter with him? A short while ago getting Lily out of his home had seemed like a good idea—a wonderful idea, in fact. Yet now he felt only reluctance at the very thought of her leaving.

For Lily's own sake, he assured himself again firmly. Because she was a visitor to his native city, and so far had not received the welcome that Roma extended to all its visitors. Nor was her brother here to spend Christmas with her, as expected. Those had to be the reasons for his current hesitation; what else could it be?

'Count Scarletti?'

The voice squawking down the earpiece of the telephone reminded Dmitri that he was still in the middle of a call.

'I will come down to the kitchen shortly,' he said to Lily, before turning in his chair to look out of the *palazzo* window while he continued his telephone call.

'I take it the work is finished?'

Lily turned from laughing at something the glazier had just translated into English for the slightly flirtatious security man, her smile fading as she saw a stony-faced Dmitri standing in the kitchen doorway, observing their conversation. 'I— No, I don't think so.' She shifted uncomfortably, aware that she had been the one distracting the two workmen.

'Then perhaps they might be allowed to get on with their work?' Dmitri suggested, as he came farther into the room to look pointedly at the other two men.

A look that obviously needed no translation, as they instantly put down their half drunk cups of coffee and hurried back to attend to the window.

Lily turned back to Dmitri. 'Wow—can you do that to a whole roomful of people?'

'Without even trying,' he drawled dryly as he walked over to the table. 'Considering I don't usually enter this part of the *palazzo*, I seem to be spending a lot of my time in here at the moment.'

She stood up to pour him a cup of coffee. 'I spend a lot of time sitting in the kitchen in my flat at home.'

'Sitting? Not cooking?' He made himself comfortable on one of the chairs around the table.

Lily put the cup down on the table before resuming her seat. 'Oh, I can cook, Dmitri.'

'You just choose not to do so while you are here,'

he acknowledged, adding neither cream nor sugar before sipping the hot brew.

Lily looked at him closely, not fooled for a minute by the apparent casualness of this conversation, and knowing that moments ago he had not been in the least happy at finding Lily and the workmen laughing together. Because she was delaying them? Or because of something else?

She gave a shrug. 'I'm a teacher, not a cook.'

He gave an inclination of his head. 'And I am sure you are a very good one.'

'Goodness me!' Lily's eyes were wide as she leant back in her chair. 'Did you just pay me a compliment?'

Dmitri frowned his irritation with her sarcasm. 'I do not believe any of my insults have been levelled at you.'

'Not personally, no. But by association, yes.'

And why should he *not* have expressed his displeasure with her brother, when he and Claudia might be the cause of the biggest scandal to rock the Scarletti family in several hundred years! 'I do not in the least blame you for your family connections, Lily,' he stated frostily.

'You could have fooled me!' An angry flush darkened her cheeks. 'And, whatever Felix may or may not have done, he will always be my twin brother, and I love him.'

They were well on their way to having another disagreement, Dmitri recognised impatiently, when all he had meant to do was apologise for his earlier abruptness by paying her a compliment. Added to which, his comment had been sincere; he was certain that her no-nonsense attitude made her an excellent teacher.

He sighed. 'I am not about to engage in another argument with you, Lily.'

'The only way that isn't going to happen is if we don't speak to each other again before I leave!' Her eyes flashed her annoyance at him.

A nerve pulsed in his cheek above his tightly clenched jaw. 'Did you remember to return your telephone call this morning?'

She looked at him blankly. 'Sorry?'

'I seem to remember that last night you promised your friend Danny that you would call him back today.' He raised dark brows.

Lily frowned; if this was his way of avoiding an argument then he was failing miserably. 'I don't think that's any of your business, Dmitri, do you?' she challenged, having no intention of telling him that she wasn't going to return Danny's call—today or any other day. That relationship was definitely over.

'As the man who was interrupted in the middle of making love to you on this table last night when you received Danny's telephone call, I think my curiosity is understandable,' he shot back.

'Would you keep your voice down?' Lily seethed across the table at him, very aware of the fact that there were two other men in the room, and that at least one of them understood English. 'I think the important word in that statement is "interrupted",' she continued with hushed fierceness. 'And it doesn't give you the right to question me about any of my friends!'

Dmitri dearly wished he had never begun this conversation. He had no idea why he had done so—except that he'd been annoyed, coming down the stairs a few minutes ago, to hear the sound of Lily's laughter mingled with the two workmen's. A light and flirtatious laugh that she had never been at ease enough to share with him.

His eyes narrowed. 'Then what *does* it give me the right to do?'

'Nothing. Absolutely nothing,' she repeated firmly, angry colour high in her cheeks. 'Now perhaps we could change the subject and you could tell me whether or not you've managed to make any progress with your telephone calls?'

He recognised her method of averting the argument by changing the subject back to Claudia and Felix. Sensible, perhaps; it had been a senseless argument in any case—one he had allowed himself to be provoked into inciting because of his curiosity about the man who had telephoned Lily so inconveniently the night before. If they had not been interrupted then Dmitri knew that he would have taken Lily on top of this table without a second thought. Without a first one, in fact.

Which perhaps explained why he was now taking his physical frustration out on her...

Perhaps. But it was not the cool, logical behaviour he usually expected of himself...

'Dmitri?'

His attention returned to Lily where she sat across the table, looking at him curiously. 'I managed to find out that Claudia hired a car at Milano airport. After that nothing has been seen of either her or your brother,' he added grimly.

Lily sighed as she slowly leant back in her chair. 'Which means they could still be in Milan.'

'Or not.'

Or not...

Lily was going to personally throttle her little brother when they finally caught up with him! If Dmitri didn't beat her to it...

CHAPTER NINE

'I can't possibly afford to stay here!' Lily squeaked, looking up, aghast, at the obviously exclusive and hideously expensive building outside where Dmitri had parked his sleek black sports car.

The hotel was only a mile or so from his home, but the journey had been long enough to show her that he drove like all the other Italians she had observed—basically without any sense or regard for traffic signals or other drivers, let alone the dozens of people who risked life and limb by travelling about on bikes and motorcycles!

Nevertheless, it was finding herself seated beside him in his expensive-smelling car, outside a hotel where she could see a doorman and several porters dealing with the luggage of chicly dressed guests going in and out of the glass front doors, which now caused the nauseous churning in her stomach—forget butterflies, they had been replaced by giant bats!

'You don't need to be able to afford to stay here,' Dmitri assured her coolly as he opened his door and got out of the car before coming round to Lily's side and opening the passenger door for her. 'Obviously you will be staying here as my guest,' he said as she made no move to get out of the car.

'There's no "obviously" about it.' She gave a stubborn shake of her head. 'Because I'm not staying here or anywhere else as the guest of Count Scarletti. I pay my own way, thank you very much.'

Dmitri felt some of his irritation drain out of him as he looked down at her stubbornly rebellious face. He was almost tempted to smile at her obvious indignation—if he had not known that any amusement at her expense would only make her more stubborn! 'At least come inside and look at the room, Lily,' he cajoled.

'There's no point in doing that when I'm not staying.' She gave another firm shake of her head as she continued to stare at the elegant façade of the hotel. 'Good Lord, Dmitri, when you said you would drive me to a hotel I didn't mean for you to take me to Rome's version of the Ritz!' She glared up at him.

This time Dmitri was unable to stop himself laughing. Lily looked so much like an indignant little bantam hen at this moment that it was impossible for him not to smile. 'Let me do this for you, Lily.' He went down on his haunches beside the open door to take one of her hands in his. 'As an apology for my boorish behaviour to date,' he explained.

Lily eyed him frustratedly. It wasn't fair that he should look so appealing boyish as he gazed at her with those warm green eyes and smiled at her so wistfully. As for that tingling sensation in her fingers and up her arm from the touch of his hands on hers...

'A verbal apology would have sufficed,' she muttered.

'This *is* my apology,' he insisted.

'It's rather an expensive one.'

'Just take a look inside, hmm?'

Could any woman resist this man when he looked so appealing? Not her, that was for certain!

She pulled her hand free of his as he stood up and stepped back to allow her to get out of the car. 'Looking doesn't mean I'm staying,' she warned as he moved to take her suitcase from the boot of the car. 'I just know I wouldn't be comfortable here.'

'Comfort is what this particular hotel is known for,' he assured her as he allowed the porter to take her suitcase from him before disappearing inside the hotel with it, thereby allowing Dmitri to take a firm grasp of her arm.

Lily didn't doubt that for a moment as she entered the hotel lobby at Dmitri's side. The marble floors and pillars were very much like those at the Palazzo Scarletti, and there was that same feeling of disembodiment from the rush and bustle of the city of Rome they had left outside.

There were a dozen or so people in the lobby—some at the discreet reception desk, others sitting in comfortable armchairs reading newspapers or looking at maps—but all turned to look as Dmitri strode through their midst, wickedly handsome, very tall for an Italian, and with his air of arrogance—

No, Lily realised slowly as she glanced up at him. Arrogance was, and always had been, the wrong word to use in association with Dmitri; arrogance implied conceit and a scorn for others that she had discovered this past day or so he simply did not possess. He was powerful, yes, and with an air of self-confidence in his own capabilities, but he wasn't in the least arrogant. Even his aloofness, his holding himself apart from others, no longer seemed to apply in regard to her...

She was becoming far too personally interested in

what did and did not make Dmitri Scarletti tick, Lily realised with a feeling of dismay.

Interested enough to resent the covetous glances he was receiving from the half dozen or so women in the lobby—old as well as young.

Far, far too interested!

He was as beyond Lily's reach as the moon, and if she had been disappointed in Danny when he'd chosen his mother over her then it was going to be nothing compared to how she was going to feel once *this* man had walked out of her life. Which, as they reached the reception desk, Lily knew was going to happen much sooner than she might have wished.

Beyond the, *'Buongiorno, signor!'* with which the brightly smiling—and very beautiful—receptionist greeted Dmitri, Lily understood none of the conversation that followed, instead turning away to allow her attention to wander around the lobby.

There was the familiar nativity scene in one corner of the spacious area—Lily had seen several others during their drive from the *palazzo*—and an eight foot tall Christmas tree in another. Its gold-and-silver decorations and harsh white lights, and several gifts neatly wrapped in silver foil beneath, made Lily long wistfully for the trees she remembered from her own and Felix's childhood.

They had usually been misshapen trees that had begun to shed their needles within days of being brought into the house by their father, with twinkling lights of different colours, and most of the decorations made during Lily and Felix's childhood, and of sentimental value only, along with the gingerbread angels and stars that they baked with their mother. The presents beneath had been wrapped untidily in gaudy paper depicting Father Christmases and snowmen, but all had somehow given the trees a much more homely appearance than the cold perfection of the tree that adorned this hotel lobby.

To Lily's consternation she felt the sharp prick of tears in her eyes just at the thought of those past Christmases with her family. Christmases so at odds with the one she was to spend alone in this impersonal hotel.

Dmitri was scowling slightly as he turned from booking Lily in and acquiring the key card to her room, knowing it was because he was very displeased with the amount of male attention she had attracted as they entered the hotel together. Even when she was dressed casually in jeans, and with a thick jacket over her sweater, her delicate blond-haired beauty was a beacon to every appreciative male gaze.

His scowl faded to concern as he looked down at her profile and saw the tears balanced precariously on her long golden lashes. 'Lily?'

She turned to look at him. 'Sorry.' She sniffed and then prompted brightly, 'All booked in?'

Dmitri wasn't fooled for a moment by her forced smile as he nodded and replaced his hand beneath her elbow to guide her across to the lifts. 'I'm sure Claudia and Felix are perfectly safe wherever they might be,' he reassured her softly as they stepped inside the mirrored lift together.

'Oh, I'm not in the least worried about that.' This time her smile was genuine.

Dmitri looked down at her searchingly. 'Then what are you worried about?'

What was she worried about? Her own unhappiness at the thought of parting from him, for one thing.

Oh, she was used to being on her own. Had been more or less on her own for the past eight years. She and Felix were close, and had usually got together once a week or so when he'd lived in London too, but nevertheless her brother had always lived his life separately from Lily, following his own star wherever it might lead him. As a consequence she had made her own life, with her own career and her own friends, and although she lived alone she had never felt lonely.

Until now…

Because of the man standing beside her. Because in a few minutes they would say goodbye and probably never meet again. Lily very much doubted that Dmitri would allow Felix or Lily anywhere near the Palazzo Scarletti again once his sister had been safely returned to him.

She felt sad just thinking about it.

Which was ridiculous, she instantly rebuked herself impatiently. Her initial opinion of Dmitri, as being an arrogant despot, might have mellowed over the past twenty-four hours, but he was still Count Scarletti—multimillionaire, and the escort of numerous beautiful and accomplished women. She very much doubted that he would give Lily Barton, a schoolteacher from England and the sister of the man he now despised, so much as a second thought once this was all over. He wouldn't even have noticed her existence at all if not for the present awkward circumstances!

'Nothing at all,' Lily denied lightly as the lift came to a halt and they stepped out into the carpeted corridor.

The place even smelt expensive, Lily acknowledged with an inner wince as her booted feet sank into the thick pile carpet and they passed several highly polished and ornate tables as they walked down the hallway. Most of them contained a vase of colourful flowers to perfume the air, and the paintings on the richly papered cream-coloured walls appeared to be originals.

As for the room—correction, *suite*—that Dmitri ushered her into seconds later...

Lily was overwhelmed by the rich elegance of the sitting room they entered, its furniture obviously antique. Several vases of yellow roses sat on tables and a large sideboard, and a bowl of assorted fruits was placed temptingly on the low coffee table in front of a leather sofa. A cut-glass chandelier hung from the ceiling, and several matching lamps were placed about the room for a more subdued lighting. And through a connecting door she could see a bedroom that was just as opulent.

'As I said earlier, Dmitri, I simply can't stay here!' Lily protested.

'Come out onto the balcony and look at the view.' Dmitri encouraged her to cross the room with him before he threw open the doors and waited for her to precede him.

Lily followed obediently, and gasped softly as she stepped out onto the balcony and found what seemed like the whole of Rome spread out before her, in all its historic and majestic beauty. And surely—surely that was St Peter's Basilica she could see across the River Tiber?

She turned to ask Dmitri if it was, only to find he had stepped back inside the suite and was even now tipping the porter who had arrived with her suitcase.

Lily turned back to the view before her, enchanted by the architecture and the sights and sounds, knowing that in that moment she'd fallen slightly in love with this magnificent city. Just as she was also falling in love with—

No! Definitely not! She would not allow herself to fall in love with the completely unattainable Dmitri Scarletti.

'Beautiful, is it not, *cara*?' he murmured appreciatively as he stepped out onto the balcony, not completely sure whether he spoke of his beloved Roma or the woman standing with her back towards him as she leant against the balcony balustrade, the glow of the platinum-gold of her hair in the sunshine appearing almost like a halo about her head before cascading onto the slenderness of her shoulders.

'Very beautiful,' she confirmed huskily without turning.

Dmitri stepped forward to rest his hands lightly on her shoulders, only to remove them again as he instantly felt her tense. 'But you still do not wish to stay here?' he guessed easily as he moved to stand beside her.

She turned and looked at him guiltily. 'Would that be very ungrateful of me?'

Dmitri felt his displeasure evaporate as he saw the uncertainty in her expression. 'Not at all,' he assured her. 'Except it would rob me of the pleasure of knowing that you are safe here, as well as comfortable.'

Her eyes widened. 'It would?'

He looked down at her from beneath hooded lids. 'Yes.'

Lily's breath seemed to have caught in her throat somewhere and it refused to be budged. The lack of oxygen was making her feel slightly light-headed as she continued to gaze up into Dmitri's pale green eyes.

In fact, she wasn't sure she could have looked away if her very life had depended on it!

Not good. *So* not good. Dangerous, in fact.

Dmitri's only reason for being concerned about her welfare had to be because Felix wasn't here with her as originally planned. Didn't it?

'I have some work to do at my office this afternoon, before we close for the Christmas holiday,' Dmitri continued before Lily could repeat her wish to leave. 'But I should like to return here at seven o'clock, if you would care to have dinner with me this evening?'

'What?' Lily just stared at him now, dumbstruck by his invitation and the possibility it opened up for her not to have to say goodbye to him just yet after all.

Dmitri smiled slightly. 'I do not believe I have ever before had that reaction to a dinner invitation.'

Probably not, Lily conceded dazedly, but she also doubted that any of the other women Dmitri had invited out to dinner were sisters of a man his own sister had eloped with!

She shook her head. 'You can't really want to waste your evening having dinner with me.'

'I would not consider it a waste of my evening.' He frowned darkly.

'I appreciate the offer, Dmitri—'

'Do you?'

'Yes. Yes, of course I do,' Lily repeated firmly, in the face of his obvious scepticism. 'But I'm sure you must have family—other than Claudia, of course…'

'Of course.' His mouth had firmed.

Lily nodded as she hastened on. 'Family, then—or possibly friends that you would rather spend Christmas Eve with?'

Dmitri shrugged those incredibly wide shoulders. 'I cannot think of any, no.'

'But—'

'Lily, it is, as you said, Christmas Eve, and I see no reason why either of us should spend it alone.' Dmitri was too irritated to attempt to hide his emotion. With both Lily and himself. Her for her hesitation in accepting his invitation. Himself for having made the invitation at all...

It would have been so much easier to rid himself of all responsibility by leaving her at this hotel and going to spend several hours in his office, before returning home to continue his search and await news of Claudia and Felix.

Easier but not, as it now turned out, what Dmitri wished to do at all.

The covetous interest of those men downstairs in the hotel lobby earlier had seriously annoyed him. Men who would no doubt approach this beautiful woman with the stunning platinum coloured hair if she were to venture downstairs alone this evening. To invite her to join one of them for a drink, perhaps. Or maybe even dinner. Invitations that the now cautious Lily would no doubt refuse, but even so...

Better by far that she have dinner with him, thereby saving her from the awkwardness of having to make those refusals.

Better by far that Dmitri did not sit at home alone this evening tormenting himself with the image of her talking and laughing with any other man!

He straightened. 'Obviously if you would prefer to be alone—'

'I didn't say that,' Lily cut in quickly, over her shock now, and certain she would prefer to spend the evening with Dmitri than anyone else. And it *was* Christmas Eve… 'But I haven't agreed to stay at this hotel yet,' she reminded him teasingly.

He quirked one dark brow. 'But you will?'

'Well…maybe for one night,' she agreed reluctantly. 'But only because I don't want to delay you any longer by putting you to the trouble of finding a less…opulent one,' she added firmly.

'Of course,' Dmitri said, secretly pleased at her capitulation. 'Is seven o'clock agreeable to you?'

Lily smiled wryly. 'I'm pretty sure I don't have any other engagements this evening.'

'Good.' He nodded his satisfaction with her answer. 'Will we be eating in the hotel or going out to eat?' Lily was frantically trying to think what she had brought with her that was suitable to wear to have dinner with Dmitri—in or out of the hotel. Nothing very exciting, that was for sure; she had packed with the idea of spending all of her time with Felix, not going out to dinner with gorgeous titled Italians!

Dmitri gave it some thought. 'I believe, as you have been in Roma for a day and a half now and seen nothing of the city, that we should go out to eat. In which case, I advise that you dress warmly.'

Which meant the little any-occasion black dress Lily had packed at the last minute, on the assumption that Felix would take her out to dinner one evening in order to introduce her to Dee, was out of the question. Or was it? Lily had also packed a warm red—very seasonal—woollen cardigan to wear over the top of it. Besides, so far in their acquaintance Dmitri had only ever seen her in jeans or tailored trousers. It would be nice if he were to realise she actually had legs. And not bad ones at that, according to some of the men she had previously dated.

Dated...?

This evening with Dmitri wasn't a *date*! He just felt sorry for her, being alone in Rome, that was all.

'Until later, then, *cara*.' Dmitri reached out to take one of her hands in his and lift it to his mouth. The firmness of his lips grazed the back of her knuckles, intent green eyes holding hers captive for several seconds before he released her and turned on his heel to go back inside the hotel room. The outer door closed softly behind him only seconds later.

While Lily remained standing on the balcony, no longer looking out at the spectacular scenery but down at her hand, where Dmitri's lips had just touched her now tingling skin...

'This is amazing!' Lily savoured a spoonful of the sharp lemon-flavoured ice cream Dmitri had just purchased for her. In a tub. Because, the vendor had informed them, cones detracted from the flavour of his magnificent ice cream.

Dmitri inclined of his head. 'I am pleased that you like it.'

Lily had enjoyed everything about this evening so far. The little restaurant where they had eaten dinner had been lovely, and Dmitri had been greeted warmly by name by the rotund proprietor. The company had been amazing and their conversation easy, the food absolutely delicious, and the red wine that accompanied it had brought a warm glow to Lily's cheeks before they had stepped back out into the enchantment that was Rome on Christmas Eve.

They had strolled along with dozens of others to a

piazza with a magnificent fountain dedicated to Neptune at its centre, where there was a busy Christmas market, with woodcutters displaying carvings of magnificent nativity scenes similar to the ones scattered about the city, and children laughing with pleasure as they took their turn on a colourful carousel.

When they'd tired of the market they had strolled on again, this time to watch people skating on an ice rink, laughing when they fell over, or beaming with pleasure when they didn't.

It had been a wonderful, magical evening, and Lily had been sure that she wouldn't be able to eat another thing after the delicious meal they had already eaten until Dmitri had taken her to the most famous ice cream parlour in Rome and purchased ices for them both from the multitude of flavours on display—lemon for Lily and chocolate for himself.

And through it all Lily had been totally aware of how disturbingly handsome Dmitri looked this evening, dressed in casual grey trousers and a grey polo-necked sweater, with a tailored black suede jacket worn over the latter, the darkness of his hair tousled by a light breeze. His several inches in height over most of his fellow countrymen added to his already distinguished air.

If Lily hadn't been completely enthralled by Dmitri before this evening, then she certainly was now. Totally. Unequivocally.

For all the good it would do her.

It was impossible for her not to be aware of the encouraging glances Dmitri received from other women—both in the restaurant and as they strolled the crowded streets of Rome. Glances he ignored for the main part, but couldn't possibly remain unaware of. From beautiful women and not so beautiful women, who all obviously had only one question in their mind: what sort of lover would the tall and handsome Italian make? Strong and masterful? Tender and attentive? Or—perfection!—a combination of the two?

Lily had found herself wondering the same thing…

Twenty-six years old, with only one very unsatisfactory lover in her past, all Lily could think about was a naked Dmitri, beside her, inside her, as the two of them shared a pleasure she had so far only imagined existed.

More ice cream! She needed to concentrate on eating more of this delicious ice cream—if only in an effort to cool herself from the eroticism of her thoughts.

Except glancing up at Dmitri from beneath lowered lashes, watching as he licked chocolate ice cream from his lips, only made Lily's inner core burn with the need to have his tongue lapping *her* in that same dedicated way.

Oh, good Lord!

Dmitri disposed of their two empty tubs and paper tissues in a bin before turning to look at Lily, frowning slightly as his gaze was drawn to and remained captured by the fullness of her pouting, rosy-coloured lips, bare of lip gloss following the eating of her ice cream, but all the more alluring because of it.

'It is almost midnight, so we have a choice as to what we do now.' His voice was terser than he had intended because of his physical awareness of her.

A tone Lily obviously recognised and misconstrued. 'Are you sure you wouldn't just rather call it a night? You've already very kindly spent the evening showing Rome to me, and—'

'That was not kindness, Lily, but pride in my city,'

he assured her lightly, determinedly dampening down his physical arousal.

An arousal that had begun the moment she had opened the door of her hotel suite to him earlier this evening. The black knee-length dress she wore fitted smoothly over her breasts and thighs, revealing slender and shapely legs, and she had two-inch-heeled strappy black shoes on her tiny feet. Her hair appeared more silver than ever against the darkness of her dress. She wore light make-up this evening—a brown mascara emphasising her long lashes, a berry-red lip gloss on the fullness of her lips the same colour as the cardigan she'd thrown about her slender shoulders before accompanying Dmitri down in the lift.

At the time it had taken all of his considerable control to resist kissing that red gloss from her sensually pouting lips. Something, he admitted with an inward wince, he was still having trouble with even without the gloss.

Lily looked up at him searchingly for several seconds, relaxing slightly as she was obviously reassured by what she saw in his guarded expression. 'What are the choices?'

He shrugged. 'There is the traditional midnight mass in St Peter's Square, or alternatively we could go and view the floodlit Trevi Fountain by moonlight.'

Lily knew exactly which one she would prefer. What woman wouldn't prefer to view the Trevi Fountain by moonlight when in the company of a man as disturbingly attractive as Dmitri? But, given her increasing awareness of him, not only was the choice a dangerous one, it also wasn't just her choice to make...

'I'm sure I'll be happy with whichever one you choose,' she said.

Dmitri smiled. 'I have attended dozens of midnight masses, but I have never seen the Trevi Fountain flood-lit or by moonlight.'

'You haven't?' Lily gasped.

His smile deepened at her obvious disbelief. 'No.'

She eyed him uncertainly. 'Are you sure you aren't just saying that because you know that I'd secretly love to visit the fountain?'

'No, I am not just saying that,' he promised. 'Have you never noticed that when you live close to something so beautiful all your life you rarely, if ever, visit it?'

'Hmm.' She smiled ruefully. 'There are parts of London I've never been to, either.'

'Exactly.' Dmitri took a light hold of Lily's arm in order to steer her through the crowded streets in the direction of the fountain, not sure if sitting beside a moonlit fountain with her was the right choice, but knowing that it was the only one he was interested in making at this moment.

She was the only woman he had really seen or been aware of all evening. The glowing blue of her eyes. The pale alabaster of her skin. The fullness of her mouth and the white evenness of her teeth when she laughed. The softness of her curvaceous body.

No, viewing the floodlit Trevi Fountain by moon-light with this beautiful woman was probably *not* the sensible choice for Dmitri to have made!

A fact born out a short time later, when they fol-lowed the sound of the cascading water to turn the street corner and see the Trevi Fountain before them in all its glory. Dozens of other couples had obviously had the same idea as them, and sat or stood together, their arms about each other, gazing at the water pouring down the lit sculptures of mermen and Pegasus and other mythological figures that made up the huge fountain, built so that it backed onto the side of a building, with a large pool of floodlit water before it.

'I had no idea!' Lily exclaimed as she came to a halt, obviously awestruck by the sheer size of the fountain as much as the sculptures themselves.

The Trevi Fountain had never been one of Dmitri's favourite examples of the beauties of Roma—he had personally always considered it as being more spectacular than truly beautiful. And yet here and now, standing beside Lily, the fountain took on a unique and inescapable beauty.

'Would you care to throw in a coin and make a wish?'

Lily dragged her gaze away from the fountain to look up at Dmitri, his face slightly in shadow from the floodlights. 'Only if you'll do the same,' she teased, very aware that she must appear like some awestruck tourist—probably because at the moment she was one! Even if it wasn't entirely the beauty of the fountain that held her mesmerised…

'Something else I have never done.' Dmitri released her arm to take some change out of his trouser pocket and hold it out to her in the palm of his hand.

Lily took one euro, waited for him to select a coin and turned back to the fountain. 'Ready? One…two…three!' She made a wish as she watched the arc of the two coins as they both flew through the air before splashing down into the beautifully clear green water.

As if on cue the bells of Rome began to ring out the midnight hour, adding to her feeling of magical disorientation, of being in a time out of time, when anything might—and could—happen.

'*Felice Natale,* Lily,' Dmitri turned to murmur at her side, as the last of the bells chimed. 'Happy Christmas, Lily,' he translated huskily.

'*Felice Natale,* Dmitri,' she responded, her own gaze caught and captured by those mesmerising green eyes.

He reached out to clasp the tops of her arms lightly before running his hands caressingly down their length. He captured her hands in his before his head slowly lowered and his lips gently claimed hers.

Lily's heart clenched in her chest as Dmitri's lips moved against hers in a slow and exploratory kiss that made her tremble from head to toe. Her hands moved out to grasp the lapels of his jacket to steady herself before slowly moving up his chest to grasp onto his shoulders. His arms came about her waist as he pulled her into the hardness of his body and their kiss deepened and lengthened.

Lily had longed but not dared to hope that Dmitri would kiss her again. She had ached with that longing all evening as her awareness of him thrummed just beneath the surface of every word spoken, every gesture made.

That awareness flared into heated arousal now, as he crushed her body against his. Their lips parted and they kissed hungrily. The hardness of his thighs was evidence of his desire as Lily's fingers became entangled in the soft and silky hair at his nape.

Both of them were breathing heavily by the time Dmitri rested his forehead against hers to look down at her with brooding intensity. 'Do not ask me to apologise for kissing you.'

'No.' Apologise? Lily wanted him to kiss her again—not apologise!

He looked down at her searchingly, a frown creasing his brow as he saw the trembling of her body. 'Are you cold?'

'I'm not trembling with the cold, Dmitri,' she admitted achingly.

'Nevertheless, it is very late.'

'Or early. Depends on your perspective.' Lily smiled briefly.

Dmitri's eyes glittered. 'You must know that I want you?'

She felt a quiver of excitement down the length of her spine at his admission. 'I—yes.' No point in being coy when their mutual arousal must be obvious to both of them!

'Will you come home with me, Lily?' Dmitri invited. 'Come back to the *palazzo* with me. Stay with me. Of your own free will this time,' he added softly.

Lily's heart leapt, her breathing ragged as she continued to look up at him. She knew exactly what Dmitri was asking, and what she would be agreeing to if she accepted his invitation; their desire was as tangible as the water that continued to cascade into the pool behind them.

If she went back to the *palazzo* with Dmitri now then Lily knew that they would end up in bed together—spend the night together with no thought of tomorrow.

Because there could be no tomorrow for the two of them. Only this one night.

But Lily wanted that so badly she physically ached with the wanting!

She moistened her lips with the tip of her tongue before answering him. 'Yes.'

His gaze heated, became molten green glass. 'Yes?'

'Yes,' she repeated with a choked laugh, wondering

at her own daring, but knowing there was no other answer she could give him.

She was in the romantic city of Rome, with the most attractive man she had ever met, and the intensity of his kisses, the heat in his gaze, the hardness of his body, were all evidence that he wanted her as much as she wanted him.

Nothing like this had ever happened to her before.

Or was ever likely to happen to her again.

It seemed that wishes made beside the Trevi Fountain really did come true, after all…

CHAPTER TEN

'It's not too late to change your mind if you're having second thoughts?'

The two of them had walked back to the *palazzo* hand in hand. Lily was lost in the euphoria of the pleasures yet to come, but she began to tremble as Dmitri had put in the code which would allow them to enter the *palazzo* by the small door set into the larger wooden doors.

A trembling he was obviously well aware of as he maintained his hold on her hand...

Did she want to change her mind?

No!

Yes!

She didn't know what she wanted!

Not true. She wanted Dmitri.

At the same time she *was* having second and third thoughts. Oh, not about wanting him. No, Lily's doubts were all about herself and her own lack of experience.

Dmitri was in his mid-thirties, had no doubt bedded dozens of beautiful women, whereas one less than satisfactory experience when she was at university—possibly such a disaster because of her own lack of expertise as much as the boy's—didn't auger well for spending the night with a man as experienced in love-making as Dmitri.

'I can take you back to your hotel if that is what you would prefer?' It was impossible for him to mistake the look of panic in her expression as she stood beside him beneath the light illuminating the doorway into the *palazzo*.

She swallowed before answering. 'Before we go in I just want you to be aware—I don't want you to be disappointed when we—I just—'

'Lily?' He turned to take both her hands in his as he looked down at her shrewdly. 'You have not done anything like this before, have you?' he asked.

'No! I mean, yes!' She gave an impatient shake of her head at the inadequacy of her reply. 'Yes, I have. But it was only the once. And it was years ago—very disappointing—and I don't want you to feel that same disappointment with regard to me,' she said desperately as she looked up at Dmitri with pained blue eyes. 'I know that you must normally…date experienced as well as beautiful women, and I'm—'

'A *very* beautiful woman,' Dmitri interjected huskily.

Her cheeks became flushed. 'That may or may not be true—'

'Oh, it is very true, Lily,' he assured her.

'But I'm not experienced,' she insisted firmly.

If Lily truly believed that information would disappoint him, then she was completely mistaken. Just the thought of being Lily's first real lover only deepened the hunger he felt to make love to her.

At the same time her revelation dispelled any lingering doubts he might have had in regard to her friendship with Danny.

'Lily.' Dmitri's hands moved up gently to cup either side of her face. 'I already know from our kisses yesterday evening and tonight that I will not be disappointed,' he murmured.

The colour deepened in her cheeks. 'You do?'

'Oh, yes.' Dmitri smiled at her encouragingly. 'And we will take this as slow or as fast as you wish it to go. Or not at all.'

'Not at all?' Lily looked up at him uncertainly, wanting to know how he knew their lovemaking wouldn't be a disappointment, but feeling too embarrassed to ask.

He nodded. 'The bedroom you used last night is still available to you if you wish it.'

Lily was completely reassured by the sincerity in his expression as he met her gaze so unwaveringly. He meant what he said. She instantly felt her nervousness fading and desire returning. 'I believe I would like to see *il padrone's* bedroom before making a decision— if that's okay with you?' she murmured.

The glitter deepened in his eyes. 'It shall be exactly as you wish it, Lily.'

This time she wasn't in the least concerned by the silence of the *palazzo* as they paused long enough in the kitchen for him to open a bottle of red wine and gather up the bottle and two glasses; in fact, she found it reassuring to know that they were completely alone here as they moved quietly through the silent hallways to Dmitri's bedroom.

Bathed in the light shining from the moon through two huge picture windows and a single golden lamp beside the bed, it was bigger and grander than any other bedroom Lily had ever seen. The deep gold-coloured carpet was so thick and luxurious the two-inch heels of her shoes sank into it completely. A low table and comfortable chairs were set in front of one of the low windows, and a long and ornate dressing table and wardrobe took up the whole of one wall. And all those things were dominated by a huge four-poster bed draped with gold curtains that matched the richness of the bedcover and half a dozen cushions arranged against the pillows.

A bedroom fit for a king.

Or an Italian count.

A man as beyond the reach of an English school-teacher as the moon was from the sun.

Even as Lily dropped her shoulder bag down onto an ornate brocade chair her nervousness returned with a vengeance!

Dmitri poured two glasses of the red wine before carrying them over to where Lily stood in the middle of his bedroom, handing her one before huskily making a toast. *'Felice, Natale.'*

Her eyes were huge as she gazed up at him. *'Felice Natale,* Dmitri.'

Dmitri watched Lily over the brim of his glass as they both sipped their wine. His own lips barely touched the ruby-red liquid, but Lily took a deep and reviving swallow as further evidence of her nervousness, which he was anxious to dispel.

He reached out to take the glass from her unresisting fingers, putting them both down on the table beside the bed before turning back to place his hands lightly against the warmth of her cheeks. 'You are so very, very beautiful, *cara,*' he murmured, and he bent down to place soft kisses against the arch of her throat. Her skin was as soft as velvet and tasted of honey and pure sensuality. A sensuality he longed to explore.

Dmitri groaned low in his throat as he continued to

cup her cheeks while his lips explored the delicate contours of her shell-like ear. He could feel her trembling and hear the soft hitch in her breathing as he bit gently on her earlobe before soothing it with his tongue.

Her hands moved up slowly, tentatively, to lie flat against his chest, her touch as light as butterfly wings through the thickness of his sweater. Dmitri held his desire for her firmly in check as he determined to dispel the last of her nervousness before he would allow his passion full rein.

A determination that crumbled into dust the moment he felt the softness of her lips against his own throat...

Lily made a soft sound as Dmitri turned and captured her mouth with his. At the same time his arms moved about her waist to gather her close against the hardness of his body. Her own lips parted in order to deepen the kiss—she needed, wanted to be as close to him as possible.

They kissed hungrily now, deeply, taking, giving, hands touching, caressing, frantic in their need to get closer than even the fragile barrier of their clothes would allow.

Lily's cheeks were flushed, her lips swollen, breasts tingling, the nipples hard and aching, and there was a burning warmth between her thighs as Dmitri broke off the kiss long enough to lift her up into his arms and carry her over to the enormous bed. He placed her down amongst the sumptuous cushions before slowly straightening to stand beside the bed, his gaze holding hers as he shrugged the jacket from his shoulders and allowed it to fall unheeded onto the carpeted floor.

His sweater came next, its removal revealing the naked width of his muscled chest and stomach and the strength of his shoulders and arms. His skin was a light and olive brown, the light dusting of hair on his chest soft and silky as it dipped beneath the waistband of the trousers he now unfastened. He slipped his feet out of his shoes before letting his trousers fall to the floor, and stepped out of them to leave himself wearing only a brief pair of body-hugging black boxers, which did nothing to hide his arousal.

Dmitri continued to look down at her as he pushed this last item of clothing down over his hips and then down his thighs. Lily gasped as her fascinated gaze was drawn to what he had revealed.

She moved to the edge of the bed on her hands and knees, inexorably drawn to taste him even as she cupped him gently.

'Dio mio...!' A groan of pleasure burst from his lips even as his hands became entangled in her hair, and he held her against him so she could take him fully into her mouth.

Dmitri felt himself swell as the intimacy of her ministrations caused the blood to course hotly through his veins. He was unable to stop himself from thrusting slowly, rhythmically, and his fingers tightened their grip in the silky tangle of her hair in an effort to draw her even closer still.

He gritted his teeth at the unimaginable pleasure she was giving him. It was almost beyond bearing!

'Basta, Lily—enough,' he finally managed to mutter as he gently pulled back from her. 'A minute—no, one second more of that and our lovemaking will be over before it has even begun,' he explained apologetically, as she looked up at him with disappointment in her eyes. 'And I have not tasted any of the delights of your own body yet,' he added gently, pulling her up onto her knees.

He discarded her cardigan, his lips against her throat as he slowly slid the zip of her dress down the length of her spine. He slipped the dress down her arms and allowed it to fall about the delicacy of her waist.

Revealing that she wore no bra beneath it!

Her breasts, small and pert, were bared to his hungry gaze—perfectly rounded orbs tipped by rose-pink nipples that were already hard and begging to be kissed.

He lowered his head and took each into his mouth in turn, his own pleasure intensified as he heard her catch her breath. Her hand cradled the back of his head to hold him against her as she arched into him, and his hand moved up to cup one breast while he caressed and tugged on the pouting nipple of the other with his mouth. Her small gasps were telling him clearly what pleased her. And he so wanted to please her!

But it was not enough. He wanted to taste all of her. He *needed* to taste all of her!

Lily offered no resistance as Dmitri disposed of her dress completely before lying her back against the silken cushions and skillfully stripping off her underwear and her shoes.

'*Bella,* Lily!' he breathed raggedly as he knelt beside her, his gaze hot as he devoured her nakedness. 'You are as beautiful, as perfect, as any Bernini sculpture.'

Lily didn't think so; she had seen the perfection of those sculptures in the guidebooks on Rome that she had devoured before coming here. But if he believed it to be true, who was she to argue?

And then she knew she couldn't have spoken, let alone argued, as Dmitri parted her legs to kneel between her thighs, the heat of his gaze centred on the jewel he had revealed amongst her silver curls before he lowered his head.

Lily exploded. That first sweet rasp of his tongue had quickly engulfed her in a pleasure unlike anything else she had ever known or imagined.

Dmitri allowed her no quarter as a second, even more intense climax hit her. Lily almost sobbed with pleasure as he brought her to peak after peak of release with his lips and tongue and those wickedly clever fingers, until she completely lost track of time and reason.

Then Dmitri entered her gently and began to move. Slowly at first—torturously slowly—before he increased the pace of his movements at her frantic entreaties, all the time murmuring words of Italian against her throat and her breasts as he kissed and caressed her, driving her ever onwards towards another peak. This time the pleasure he gave her seemed to come from the very depths of her, and she clung on to his shoulders mindlessly as he took her with him to his own plateau and then over the edge into oblivion.

Dmitri woke slowly, pleasurably, aware of the morning sunlight of winter shining through the windows as he lay curled spoon-fashion against the back of the woman asleep beside him in the bed, her hair a silken curtain of platinum down the length of her back. One of his arms was draped across her waist, and her hand was over his as he cupped the fullness of her breast. His morning arousal nestled snugly against the curve of her bottom.

Lily.

Beautiful Lily.

He had never encountered a more giving and responsive lover. He didn't just think so; he *knew* so!

Despite having awakened her in the early hours of the morning to make love a second time, Dmitri knew that he wanted her again. *Now.*

As if she was aware of his need, he felt her stir in his arms, and knew the exact moment when she came completely awake. His breath left him in a heartfelt sigh as she parted her legs invitingly, to allow him to enter her inch by slow inch, their movements languid, measured, as they brought each other to another satisfying climax.

It was difficult for Dmitri to know which was the more satisfying—the wild and lusty lovemaking of last night, or the gentle giving and taking of this morning. Both had been unique and exciting in a way he had never imagined.

'Sorry to introduce the mundane, Dmitri.' Her self-conscious chuckle reverberated against his chest. 'But I believe I need to use the bathroom.' She turned to look at him teasingly over one bare shoulder.

He kissed her lingeringly, smiling as he slowly withdrew from her and lay back on the pillows. 'And while you are gone I will go downstairs to make us breakfast, and bring it up on a tray so that we can eat it together in bed.'

'No one has ever brought me breakfast in bed before,' Lily murmured as she rolled over to lean on her elbows and look down at him, still slightly dazed at being in bed with the deliciously gorgeous and totally edible Dmitri Scarletti. Dazed and satiated. More than she would ever have believed possible before the wonders of last night and this morning.

Nevertheless, she still felt slightly shy when she thought of the intimacies they had shared, her cheeks warming as she recalled how she had touched, caressed and kissed his body, and how he had reciprocated.

Dmitri reached up to smooth the hair at her temple. 'Every woman should be brought breakfast in bed on Christmas morning, *cara*.'

Oh, good Lord—it was too! Lily had totally forgotten it was Christmas Day in the glowing aftermath of their lovemaking. 'I don't have a gift for you.' She gave a rueful shake of her head.

'Nor I you.' His eyes were warm with laughter. 'But I believe we might think of certain gifts we can give each other once our strength has been restored with food, hmm?'

Lily became lost in the dizzying fact that they had known each other for less than two days. Certainly when they had met she would never have imagined that they would end up in bed together this morning!

Dmitri sat up to kiss her lingeringly on the lips. 'And later—much, much later,' he added huskily, 'we will discuss what you would like to do with the rest of the day.'

Lily's breath caught in her throat as she looked at him searchingly. Had she been wrong? Hadn't this just been a one-night stand for him? He obviously wanted to spend the rest of the day with her too…

His next words confirmed it, as his lips sent rivulets of pleasure down her spine as he sought the hollows of her throat. 'Today will just be for you and me, *cara*.' He bit gently on her earlobe and chuckled when she arched her back in pleasure. 'A feast to satisfy all our senses.'

His words conjured up such a vivid image of Dmitri eating sliced strawberries from the tips of her breasts, drinking their juice from her navel, that Lily once again felt deliciously aroused.

'It sounds...wonderful,' she breathed longingly.

'Oh, it will be, *cara.*' Dmitri kissed her one last time before throwing back the bedclothes to stand beside the bed, totally unselfconscious in his own nakedness as he padded softly across the carpeted floor towards the bedroom door.

Lily lay back on the bed, totally relaxed as she enjoyed that unobstructed view of the lean contours of his back and the tautness of his bottom.

Was a man supposed to have such a gorgeous bottom that it tempted a woman to want to bite it? Whether he was or not, that was exactly what she wanted to do to it!

Later. She could do as she wished later.

She stretched as he left the room, becoming lost in sensual and arousing memories as her body ached in places she hadn't known it could ache. Pleasurable, hidden places that had known the touch of Dmitri's lips and hands, and caresses that now made her blush to think of them. Or flush with excitement at the thought of him repeating them!

It was the sound of the telephone ringing somewhere in the distant reaches of the *palazzo* that finally penetrated her daydreams, reminding her that he would be returning soon and she hadn't even gone to the bathroom yet.

She would have time later to indulge in yet more fantasies...

Dmitri hadn't come back upstairs by the time Lily returned, refreshed, from the bathroom, having lingered long enough to take a quick shower as well as brush her teeth. The black silk robe she had found hanging behind the door was obviously one of Dmitri's, and it reached to her ankles when she slipped in on over her nakedness. She'd had to turn the sleeves back three times in order to free her hands so that she could wrap the robe about her twice before tying the belt in place.

It might not be glamorous, but it definitely felt sexy. The silky material brushed softly over her sensitised breasts and thighs much like the caress of Dmitri's lips and fingers, causing Lily's nipples to stand erect and engorged beneath it.

She wandered over to the window to look out over the city of Rome. A city that would forever be the most romantic in the world as far as she was concerned. The city where she had fallen in love—

She turned as she heard the sound of the door opening, smiling teasingly as she saw he wasn't carrying the promised tray of food and drinks. 'Did you decide that breakfast could wait, after all—' She abruptly broke off her teasing, the smile freezing on her lips as she became aware of the bleakness of Dmitri's expression.

His jaw was clenched, his mouth a thin, uncompromising line, and his eyes glittered like shards of pale green glass in the pallor of his face. He totally ignored Lily's presence in his bedroom as he moved to pull on black boxers before dressing quickly in jeans and a black sweater taken from the shelves in the long wardrobe.

'Dmitri?' Lily was alarmed as she crossed the width of the bedroom in light, hesitant steps. 'Dmitri, is everything all right?'

He turned sharply, and she recoiled slightly from the icy anger she could see those chilling green eyes. 'Of course everything is not all right!' he said cuttingly.

Lily gave a gasp as she fell back a step, her cheeks paling in the face of his obvious disgust.

Oh, dear Lord! Could it be that in the clear light of day he had gone downstairs and realised exactly who he had shared his bed with the previous night?

And wished that he hadn't...

CHAPTER ELEVEN

DMITRI'S eyes narrowed as he saw Lily's stricken expression. 'Did you imagine that I would be pleased about the situation?' he bit out furiously.

Her eyes were wide. 'I— Well— No, perhaps not pleased, exactly. But—'

'There is no *but,* Lily.' Dmitri began to pace the bedroom, feeling much like a confined tiger must as it paced its cage. He needed to get out of here. Away from Lily who looked so sexily alluring in his own black silk bathrobe. And the memories the rumpled bedclothes behind her brought so vividly back to mind. 'I will wait for you to join me downstairs in the kitchen once you are dressed and we will discuss this there,' he informed her frostily.

'Discuss it?' She gave a frantic shake of her head. 'Oh, no, Dmitri. I don't think I want to sit down with you and actually talk about…about what's happened!' She looked horrified at the suggestion.

His eyes narrowed. 'Because our opinions on the situation differ so drastically?'

Lily swallowed hard. 'No doubt,' she said faintly, wondering if the pain in her chest was caused by the fact that she couldn't seem to breathe properly or if her heart might actually be breaking into a million pieces.

Because she had realised during Dmitri's absence downstairs that it wasn't only the city of Rome she had fallen in love with last night but that she loved Dmitri deeply. Completely. Irrevocably...

And he was looking at her, talking to her, as if last night had been nothing but a mistake on his part. A mistake he obviously deeply regretted.

She looked away, no longer able to bear even looking at the disgust she could so easily read in his expression. 'I think it best if I just get dressed and then go straight back to the hotel.'

'Where no doubt you will order a bottle of champagne and drink a toast to the happy couple?' he said accusingly.

Lily turned back slowly. 'I'm sorry—I don't understand?'

Dmitri snorted. 'I am sure Felix was only too delighted to explain the situation to you!'

'Felix?' She frowned. 'But—'

'I am not in the mood to play games, Lily.' Dmitri eyed her coldly. 'Claudia told me that Felix was telephoning you at the same time as she spoke to me. I thought it best not to tell her that at that moment you were upstairs in my bedroom.' His mouth twisted. 'But please do not attempt to pretend you do not know exactly what I am talking about.'

'I don't.' Lily stared up at him uncomprehendingly. 'I did hear the telephone ringing downstairs earlier, but— That was Claudia?'

'Oh, yes,' he said from between clenched teeth.

Lily's throat moved as she tried to swallow, her mouth suddenly very dry. 'I went into the bathroom while you were downstairs. I took a shower.' She shook her head. 'I haven't heard from Felix since before I left

London, apart from that message he left on my mobile two days ago telling me to not come to Rome after all.' Something Lily dearly wished she hadn't done now!

If she had never come to Rome then she would never have met Dmitri. Never have fallen in love with him!

He became very still, his eyes narrowed as he looked down at her. 'Is this true?' he asked.

'I don't tell lies, Dmitri,' Lily assured him tightly. 'Felix may have tried to call me,' she continued dully. 'But as he still has no idea that I didn't receive his message two days ago and that I actually came to Italy, I doubt he will have been successful.' She took her mobile out of her bag, where it sat on the chair where she had dropped it the night before in her eagerness to be in Dmitri's arms. In his bed! 'As I thought—there are no missed calls.' She held her mobile up in front of Dmitri's face, so that he could see from the lit display that she wasn't lying.

'Dannazione!' A nerve pulsed in his clenched jaw.

'Exactly,' Lily agreed, pretty sure the curse wasn't lost in the translation. 'And as you seem to know the reason for Felix wanting to speak to me perhaps you wouldn't mind enlightening me?'

Dmitri's nostrils flared briefly. 'As we suspected, Claudia and Felix flew onto another destination after arriving in Milano. To Las Vegas, to be exact. Where it appears they got married yesterday.'

Lily had guessed what Dmitri was going to say before he'd said it—oh, not about Las Vegas specifically, but about the marriage. Even so, hearing the actual words was still enough of a shock for her to stagger backwards before sitting down heavily on the side of the bed.

Claudia and Felix were married!

Dmitri's present anger might not be about the night the two of them had spent together, after all, but Lily could hardly believe that her little brother was now a married man, another woman's husband. She was filled with happiness for Felix, of course, and yet at the same time aware of a deep sense of loss inside herself, along with an awareness of her own relationship with her twin changing, shifting. They were no longer Felix and Lily but now Felix and Claudia, and Felix's sister Lily.

It was…strange, to say the least. Would take a little time to adjust to.

Time the icily furious expression on Dmitri's face told her he wasn't about to give her!

Lily breathed out shakily. 'You're right, Dmitri. Perhaps it would be better if we discussed this downstairs once I've dressed.'

He looked down the length of his aristocratic nose at her. 'When no doubt our views on the subject will differ greatly!'

She gave him a rueful smile.

He didn't return it. 'Do not take too long. There are obviously telephone calls I now need to make.'

'To Francesco Giordano for one,' she muttered.

He stiffened. 'I believe any contact with the Giordano family can wait until Claudia returns to Roma and I have a chance to talk with her.'

'Attempt to bully her into ending her marriage to Felix, don't you mean?' Lily suggested furiously.

He glowered at her. 'Do you disagree that they are totally mismatched?'

She gave a weary sigh as she stood up. 'I'm sure that my views on the subject will have little or no impact on what you intend to do or not do about it.'

'At least we are in agreement on something!' Dmitri snapped before swiftly leaving the bedroom.

Lily's heart felt heavy in her chest as she watched him go, knowing that it was probably the last thing that they would ever agree on...

Dmitri's displeasure at the knowledge of his sister's clandestine marriage hadn't dissipated in the slightest by the time a pale-faced Lily joined him downstairs in the kitchen of the *palazzo*, ten minutes later.

Although the fact that she was once again dressed in the black knee-length dress and red cardigan from yesterday evening was a stark reminder of the fact that he had spent the night here in bed with her rather than returning her to the hotel.

It was a night that Dmitri knew he would never forget.

It was the first time he had spent a whole night in bed with any woman. The first time he had intended to spend the whole day with a woman too. But that certainly wasn't going to happen now.

His mouth tightened. 'I forgot to ask earlier how your hand is this morning.'

'I told you—I heal quickly.' She gave a small shrug as she held up her hand. Only a small plaster now covered the cut she had received after breaking the kitchen window two days ago.

'Would you care for a cup of coffee while we talk?'

Lily looked across at him guardedly. 'I don't see what there is for us to talk about.' She sighed heavily. 'Claudia and Felix are both over twenty-one, they're married and that would appear to be the end of it.' It was certainly the end of Lily's own dreams—ridiculous, romantic dreams, she accepted now—of there being any sort of future for Dmitri and herself. At the moment he looked as if he would like to strangle with his bare hands anyone even remotely related to Felix; as his twin, she didn't stand a chance!

He bared his teeth in a humourless smile. 'I am sure Claudia and Felix are both under the impression that it is the beginning, not the end!'

Lily's chin rose at the sinister undertones of that statement. 'Which is exactly what it is.'

Dmitri's nostrils flared. 'Not if I have anything to say about it.'

'Which you don't,' Lily said firmly.

His mouth tightened. 'Do not underestimate me, Lily. As I warned you once before, until Claudia comes into her inheritance at the age of twenty-five I retain the power to disinherit her.'

Lily frowned. 'And is that what you intend doing?'

Dmitri eyed her pityingly. 'How long do you suppose her new husband will remain at her side if she is no longer the wealthy Claudia Scarletti?'

'I believe you will find she is now Claudia Barton,' Lily corrected tightly. 'And perhaps you shouldn't underestimate Felix, Dmitri. No matter what you may choose to think to the contrary, I don't believe my brother would have married Claudia if he wasn't deeply in love with her.'

His mouth twisted derisively. 'What a little romantic you are, Lily!'

'And what a cynic *you* are!' She felt stung into retaliating.

'Any man in my position would feel cynical—'

'And what position is that?' Lily challenged.

'I am the older brother of an impressionable young

girl who has been seduced into marrying a penniless Englishman!' Dmitri thundered wrathfully.

Lily felt the warmth of anger in her cheeks. 'That "penniless Englishman" happens to be my brother!'

'I am well aware of who he is, Lily. And *what* he is,' he added coldly.

She became very still. 'Oh? And what's that?'

'A fortune hunter, of course,' Dmitri accused. 'Nothing but a—'

'I'm not going to remain here and listen to you insult my brother any further,' Lily cut in, and she turned away.

'You will remain here until I say otherwise—'

'No, Dmitri, I won't,' she insisted as she glared across at him, her back rigid with indignation. 'And if I have to break another window in order to get out of here then that's exactly what I'll do,' she warned fiercely.

Dmitri drew in a long and steadying breath, aware of his loss of the temper he was usually at such pains to keep firmly under his control. But what man would *not* lose his temper upon learning that his only sister, and one who had been more like his own child than a sibling, had not only married without any of her family present, thousands of miles away from home, but to add insult to injury had married a man he knew only as his employee, and certainly did not approve of as a husband for her?

He looked across at Lily, knowing by the indignant stiffness of her body, and the way her knuckles showed white as her hand tightly gripped the strap of her shoulder bag that she meant exactly what she said.

Surprisingly, this evidence of her righteous indignation on her brother's behalf helped to calm some of his own anger. He sighed heavily. 'I do not believe us resorting to insults will in any way help to solve this dilemma.'

'No?' Lily said. 'That didn't seem to stop you doing exactly that a few minutes ago!'

His mouth thinned. 'I apologise if you found offence in anything I said just now.'

Lily wasn't offended. She was way beyond offended. She was hurting so badly that if she didn't soon get out of here she was afraid she was going to burst into loud, uncontrollable sobs. Which would only complete her humiliation...

Wasn't it bad enough that she had spent the night with this man, made love with him in ways that made her blush even to think of them, *and* fallen in love with him, without having to listen to him insulting her brother—and thereby her too? Of course it was! 'Keep your apology, Dmitri,' she said. 'And just let me out of here.'

'No.'

Her eyes widened at his refusal. 'What do you mean, *no*? Oh, don't tell me,' she continued scornfully. 'You now intend to once again keep me a prisoner here, until Felix returns Claudia to you and you can have their marriage annulled!'

His mouth compressed. 'Considering that they were married yesterday, on Claudia's birthday, I am sure it is a little late for an annulment.'

Lily gave a pained wince at the obvious fact that even if Claudia and Felix hadn't slept together before their marriage then they would certainly have done so now! 'So what's the plan, Dmitri?' She eyed him curiously. 'Do you perhaps intend to attempt to buy Felix off? And if that doesn't work go ahead with your earlier idea of disinheriting Claudia?' She snorted. 'Before you do anything too rash, I think you should seriously stop and think how Claudia will react, and how you might irrevocably damage your own relationship with her.'

A nerve pulsed in his tightly clenched jaw. 'For one thing, I have no intention of setting a precedent by attempting to buy off a fortune hunter. Secondly, I am fully aware that Claudia will be…less than pleased if I intercede.'

'From what you've told me of your sister, I think you'll find that her emotions might go a little deeper than "less than pleased"!' Lily said incredulously.

His mouth tightened. 'Nevertheless, I hope that she will eventually come to realise that I have acted only in her best interests.'

'And if she doesn't?'

Dmitri looked bleak. 'Then at least I will have the satisfaction of *knowing* that I acted only in her best interests.'

'And will that be enough for you?' she asked gently.

His nodded. 'It will have to be.'

Lily sighed deeply. 'All I can tell you is that if Felix so much as dared even to try and interfere in my life in that way, then I'd tell him to go to hell—after I'd punched him on his arrogant nose, of course.'

Hell was pretty much where Dmitri felt he was at this moment.

Definitely caught between a rock and a hard place. Damned if he did and damned if he didn't.

But there was no way he could simply stand back and accept his sister's hasty marriage to Felix Barton without challenge.

As for his own brief relationship with Lily… She was so angry with him at this moment that she would most likely administer that punch to *his* arrogant nose if he so much as broached the subject of the night they had just spent together!

'I will bear your advice in mind.'

'Oh, it wasn't advice, Dmitri,' she insisted. 'If Claudia is half the woman you've implied she is then you would do well to tread very carefully in how you choose to deal with your disapproval of her marriage.'

Dmitri was well aware of that; he was just too stunned at this moment to be able to think logically about the subject.

Or about how he and Lily were to proceed now. If they were to proceed at all...

'What are you own immediate plans?'

'My immediate plans?' The evenness of her tone did nothing to lessen the anger glittering in her deep blue eyes. 'I believe I've already told you that I intend going back to the hotel—not to drink champagne, as you suggested earlier,' she said, 'but to check out and pay my bill. I'll find somewhere cheaper to stay until I can get a flight back to England.'

Dmitri stiffened. 'I have told you that I intend to pay for your hotel—'

'And I'm now telling *you* that under the circumstances I can't allow you to do that,' she cut in firmly.

His eyes narrowed to glassy slits. 'And what circumstances are those?'

She met his gaze bravely. 'Do you really need me to spell it out for you?'

No, he didn't require any explanation, Dmitri realised ruefully. He knew from the anger in her expression that by leaving the hotel she was firmly stating that she refused to accept any further assistance from him. A clear indication that she wished to have nothing more to do with the man with whom she had spent the previous night, who minutes ago had insulted her brother in the worst possible way...

But Claudia was Dmitri's sister—his beloved younger sister for whom he had cared for since she was six years old. What else could he do but try to salvage something from the mess he believed she had now made of her life?

Even if by doing so he risked his own relationship with Claudia?

Yes, even then!

Even if it brought to an end any possibility of a relationship between himself and Lily?

It was already at an end, he accepted heavily as he saw the distaste in Lily's expression. 'I will drive you to your hotel—'

'I don't think so, thank you,' she refused. 'I would prefer to get a taxi.'

'That is totally impractical—'

'But necessary,' she assured him fiercely.

'I was referring to the fact you will not find too many taxis in service on Christmas Day,' he explained. 'Even in Rome.'

My God, it *was* Christmas Day, Lily accepted bleakly; she had once again forgotten that fact. It was rapidly escalating into being the worst of her entire life. And to think that last night, and again earlier this morning, she had believed it to be the best one...

What a difference a single telephone call could make—especially when it had been intended to herald good news rather than bad.

But Dmitri had made it more than obvious that he would never approve of Claudia and Felix's marriage.

And he would never see Lily now as being anything other than Felix's sister…

'Then I'll walk back,' she announced. 'It isn't far, and the fresh air will do me good.'

Dmitri breathed his frustration with her stubbornness. 'Claudia and Felix are planning to fly back to Italy in the next few days.'

'I thought perhaps they might.'

His eyes narrowed. 'You do not intend to stay in Roma until they return?'

Lily had thought about it—she had determinedly thought of nothing else as she'd hastily dressed before coming downstairs. Thinking about the night she had just spent in Dmitri's arms would only have resulted in tears, and she fully intended saving them until she was in the privacy of her hotel room.

And so she had concentrated on Felix. On what she should do next.

Even when they were children Lily had always been the responsible one. The one who had always defended Felix and bailed him out of whatever mischief he had got himself into. That responsibility had intensified after their parents died. But his marriage to Claudia Scarletti was so much bigger than that; he was a married man now, with all the responsibilities that entailed. It was time that Lily stepped back and allowed Felix to deal with those responsibilities himself.

Besides which, she was absolutely positive that he wouldn't gain Dmitri's respect or approval by hiding behind his older sister's skirts!

No, she would give Felix her verbal support and good wishes when next she spoke to him, but other than that she had decided she must leave it to him to fight his own battles from now on—in this particular case for both his marriage and his wife.

She shrugged. 'I think it best if I go back to England on the next available flight.'

Dmitri scowled his displeasure at the idea, even though he realised it was inevitable that she would leave Italy eventually.

They had said all that they had to say to each other—possibly more than they should have said. Circumstances dictated that all that remained was for them to say goodbye…

'That is your own choice, of course,' he said stiffly.

'Most of my decisions are,' Lily said dryly. 'Thank you for helping to make my stay in Rome such an… interesting one.'

Dmitri studied her through narrowed lids. 'It is ridiculous that we should part in such a stilted way—'

'Ridiculous, but necessary,' Lily cut in, knowing that she'd suffered enough heartache for one morning. For a lifetime, in fact! Which was probably how long it was going to take her to get over loving Dmitri. 'If you would just key in the code to open the front door, I can see myself out,' she added.

'Lily—'

'Will you just do it, Dmitri?' She turned on him fierily, eyes blazing, angry colour in her cheeks.

He drew in a sharp breath. 'You do realise that if I do not manage to convince Claudia as to the unsuitability of her marriage to Felix then you and I will meet again? If not before, possibly at the christening of their first child.'

Lily gave a humourless smile. 'That's always supposing that Claudia is speaking to you again by then.'

'Which is a big assumption on my part,' Dmitri acknowledged fairly.

The fact that he now seemed to be accepting that it might very well come to that was a step in the right direction as far as Lily was concerned; she was sure that the very last thing Felix wanted was to be the cause of a serious—possibly permanent—rift between Claudia and her brother.

As to Lily and Dmitri ever meeting again...

Just the thought of having to suffer him behaving towards her and looking at her as if she were a stranger to him—as if they'd never met, let alone spent the night in bed together making love, was enough to twist Lily's insides into painful knots.

'We'll have to cross that bridge when—or if—we come to it,' she said briskly. 'Right now I think the most important thing is for me to go back to my hotel and leave you to get on with whatever Machiavellian plan you're hatching in order to separate Felix and Claudia once they're back in Rome.'

Dmitri scowled his displeasure at her description. 'You make me sound like a monster, when all I am trying to do is protect my much younger sister.'

'A sister who obviously no longer believes herself to be in need of your protection,' Lily pointed out. 'And I really don't think it's *my* opinion of you that you should be worrying about right now.'

Possibly not—and yet Dmitri found that he didn't care to have Lily leave the *palazzo,* leave Italy, thinking so badly of him. 'There is no reason why I cannot continue to show you Roma for the remainder of your stay here.'

'Now you're the one who's being ridiculous!' Lily

stared up at him incredulously, not in the least perturbed by the nerve pulsing in his tightly clenched jaw.

'I fail to see why we cannot continue to behave in a civilized manner towards each other, at least.'

'Then you must be singularly insensitive!' she snapped. 'I don't believe you,' she continued. 'Here I am, trying to leave the *palazzo* with a little of my dignity still intact, and you're suggesting we go sightseeing together!' She ran an agitated hand through her hair.

He looked down the long length of his nose at her. 'I see no reason for your dignity, or my own, to be in the least affected by what occurred last night.'

'Maybe that's exactly the reason I need to leave here!' Lily said under her breath.

Dmitri's mouth tightened. 'We did not do anything of which we need to feel ashamed.'

'I'm not ashamed—just mortified by the whole embarrassing episode! Now, unless you want me to try and kick my way out of here, I suggest you make sure the front door is open by the time I get there!'

She gave him one last sweeping glance before turning to march out of the kitchen, the heels on her shoes tapping a tattoo as she continued down the hallway to the door that led out into the courtyard. She closed it behind her with finality a few seconds later.

Dmitri felt numb as he crossed the kitchen to where the security pad was attached to the wall. He keyed in the code to open the front door, knowing by the determined expression on Lily's face as she'd left that she was quite capable of carrying out her threat to try and kick the door down if it wasn't open when she got there, and not wishing her to injure herself in the attempt.

Just as he had hurt her earlier, with his response to Claudia and Felix's marriage?

For once in his life Dmitri had no answers. Either to that question or to exactly what had taken place between himself and Lily last night. The 'embarrassing episode', as she had just called it.

And nor had he ever felt quite so alone as he did now that she had walked so completely out of his life...

CHAPTER TWELVE

London, two weeks later.

'LILY?'

It was late—almost six o'clock—and Lily was huddled down in her thick black ankle-length overcoat in order to keep out the freezing cold January winds that blew leaves and other debris about her feet as she hurried in the darkness to where she had parked her car that morning when she'd arrived for work. She came to an abrupt halt on hearing the sound of her name being spoken huskily, instantly recognising that all-too-familiar voice.

She turned quickly, her gaze apprehensive as she searched the darkness of the car park and her breath catching in her throat as she saw a tall figure separate itself from a car parked beneath some trees a short distance away from her own. A dark and menacing-looking figure that, despite the voice, might or might not be Dmitri.

Lily had imagined she had seen him so many times during the two weeks since she had flown back from Rome. Several times walking along the busy London streets. Outside her apartment building. Once even outside the school. Another time at the supermarket—as if! And all of those sightings had turned out to be of men who were just tall and dark-haired, and nothing at all like Dmitri once she had seen their faces.

Except this time there was the voice...

'Who's there?' she prompted warily, shoulders hunched inside her coat and her red woollen hat pulled low over her brow to keep out the cold. She was very aware of the fact that she had been the last to leave the school building—with a long evening on her own in her apartment to look forward to, there hadn't seemed any reason to hurry home. She and this man were alone here in the darkness of the school car park.

The man stepped out from beneath the shelter of the trees, his face still remaining partly in shadow from the clouds shrouding the moon overhead. 'It's only been two weeks, Lily. Surely you haven't forgotten me already?'

Her breath left her lungs in a whoosh as she realised it really was Dmitri. Only he had the power to rob her completely of breath and make her heart rate speed up to twice its normal speed at the same time!

What on earth was he doing here?

Lily had returned to London after managing to secure a seat on a flight back to England the day after Boxing Day. Since then she had begun to wonder if her time in Italy with Dmitri had all been nothing but a dream. A wonderful, exciting dream, but a dream nonetheless.

She swallowed hard, her shoulders tensed as she faced him across the car park. 'What are you doing here, Dmitri?'

He shrugged wide shoulders inside the heavy dark overcoat he wore, the collar turned up to ward off the icy winds. 'I was in London on business, and Claudia thought it would be nice if I stopped by and said hello to you while I'm here,' he said.

Claudia had thought it would be nice. Not Dmitri.

And, having now met her sister-in-law—Claudia and Felix had flown over to London purposely the previous week, so that the two women might meet and get to know each other—she very much doubted that the spirited Claudia had put the suggestion quite as mildly as Dmitri wished to imply she had.

Claudia was everything that both men had said she was: beautiful, sweet, innocent—and single-mindedly determined when it came to having her own way. Lily had loved the other woman from their very first meeting! The fact that Claudia obviously adored Felix went a long way to furthering those feelings of affection.

Lily gave a rueful smile. 'Well, now that you have you can go back to Italy with a clear conscience. If you'll excuse me…? It's cold out here, and I would like to go home and have something warm to eat.'

Dmitri strolled across the car park until he stood only feet away from her, his teeth gleaming briefly in the darkness as he returned her smile. 'If that was an invitation to join you at your apartment for dinner, then I accept.'

'I— But— You and I both know it was no such thing!' Lily glared at him.

Of course he knew that; it was all too obvious from her defensive attitude that she was far from pleased to see him again. Which was a pity, because he was very pleased to see her…

Not that he could see her all that well in this dark and deserted car park, with even the silver gilt of her hair covered by a woollen hat, but he could hear the softness of her voice, and smell her perfume.

Dmitri could also see that despite her heavy coat and that woollen hat she was shivering slightly from the icy cold winds. 'Perhaps you're right, and it would be better if we saved all conversation until we are at your apartment.'

'I don't believe I said that, either. Let go of me, Dmitri!' she protested as his fingers curled purposely about the top of her arm and he turned her in the direction of his hire car.

He raised dark brows. 'You would prefer that we continue this conversation out here in the cold?'

Her eyes flashed in the darkness as she defiantly stood her ground. 'I would prefer that we not continue this conversation at all! You've done your duty, Dmitri, now just—'

'My being here has absolutely nothing to do with duty!' he cut in harshly, at the same time turning her to grasp both of her arms and shake her slightly. 'I know that we parted badly in Roma, Lily, but do you really hate me so much now that you cannot bear to be anywhere near me?'

Lily gaped up at him. Hate him? How on earth could she possibly hate him when she loved him so much she had thought of nothing else but him for the past two weeks? The husky sound of his voice. The way he smiled. The way he laughed. The way he moved. The touch of his hands. The soft demand of his lips. The way he had made love to her so passionately the one night they had spent together...

Hate Dmitri? Lily could never, ever do that.

But nor did she intend to make a complete fool of herself by putting herself in the position of ever allowing Dmitri to see how much she loved him. And being alone with him in her apartment would do it! 'This is a ridiculous conversation at best,' she declared tautly. 'A waste of time at worst.' She shook her head. 'We said all that we had to say to each other that last morning in Rome.'

Dmitri drew his breath in sharply at her accusing tone. He had relived that last conversation with her over and over again in his mind. And each time he had done so he had realised how badly he had behaved. Admittedly he had been angry and upset after Claudia's telephone call telling him of her hasty marriage, but that was no excuse for the way he had talked to Lily afterwards, or the way in which they had parted so acrimoniously.

He looked down at her searchingly in the darkness, although he couldn't really make out her expression. 'Do you really believe that, Lily?'

'Don't you?' she came back defensively.

If he did then he wouldn't be here now... 'Is the night we spent together the reason that you are refusing to attend Claudia and Felix's service of blessing on Saturday?'

Lily drew her breath in sharply at the directness of this attack.

Of course it was the reason she had refused to attend the service on Saturday! Not that she had put it in quite that way the night before when she had told Felix on the telephone that she wouldn't be there. No, she had told her brother that she couldn't leave England again at the moment, having only just started the new term at school after the Christmas holidays. A feeble excuse that Dmitri, at least, had seen straight through!

Her chin rose. 'As I explained to Claudia and Felix,

I can't disappear off to Rome again so soon after starting the new school term.'

'Not even to attend your own brother's marriage blessing?'

Lily's mouth firmed. 'No, not even then.'

Although it would break her heart not to be there. But seeing Dmitri again, having him either look straight through her or being forced to be socially polite to her because of Claudia and Felix, wouldn't just break her heart, it would destroy it utterly. Although the fact that Dmitri was here now rather nullified that reasoning, didn't it?

'Maybe I'll reconsider,' she sighed.

'I think that would be a wise decision.'

She looked at him sceptically. 'I can't see why it should matter to *you* whether or not I come to the blessing after the way you reacted to there being a marriage at all!'

Dmitri gave a humourless smile. 'I have you to thank for helping to change my mind on the subject.'

'Me?' Her eyes widened. 'What on earth did I have to do with anything?'

He sighed heavily. 'Our last conversation together. The harsh realities you pointed out to me then made me realise that by being so intransigent over the marriage I ran the risk of losing Claudia for ever.'

'Oh?'

'Yes,' he admitted bluntly. 'So much so that by the time Claudia and Felix arrived back in Roma I had thought the situation through properly and decided that, although I still have my doubts about the marriage, Claudia is over twenty-one, and it is not up to me to decide her future for her.'

'Oh.' Lily sounded even more deflated by his added explanation.

He smiled again in the darkness. 'With that in mind, I suggested that the two of them have a blessing in Roma—'

'*You* suggested it?'

'Yes,' he confirmed. 'Not only do Claudia's other relatives and friends need that evidence of their marriage, but I need it.'

'The Giordano family too?' Lily asked tentatively.

Dmitri shrugged. 'They are less than pleased at both the marriage and my own prevarications, of course. But no doubt they will get over it in time.'

No doubt—if Count Dmitri Scarletti had anything to do with it!

'I have decided to transfer Felix to my offices in Milano next month, as a way of bringing him further into the management of the Scarletti Corporation. It means that Felix and Claudia will both have to move to Milano, of course, but the manager there is retiring at the end of the year, and if Felix proves himself capable then he will take over when Augusto retires.'

'Wow—you *have* had a change of heart,' Lily breathed softly.

'It was as you said—I either changed, adapted to the circumstances being as they are and not as I wish them to be, or I risked alienating Claudia for ever. I chose the lesser of the two evils,' Dmitri added dryly.

'That sounds more like the Count Dmitri Scarletti that I remember,' Lily teased.

'Indeed,' he drawled. 'Now, do you think we could get out of this freezing cold weather and go to your home and talk?'

Lily wished she could see him better than the single

lamp and moonlight allowed. He certainly sounded sincere enough—not going so far as to say he approved of Claudia and Felix's marriage, but not deliberately trying to destroy it, either. It was quite a concession on his part, considering his earlier vehemence on the subject.

She made her mind up quickly. 'Okay.' She nodded. 'But I don't suggest either of us leaves our cars here overnight to get stolen or vandalised, so you'll have to follow me.'

'Gladly,' he murmured.

Lily gave him one last guarded glance before hurrying over to her car and unlocking it before getting quickly inside. Only to lean back against the seat for several seconds as she tried to take in the fact that Dmitri was really here. That he was coming back to her apartment with her.

That he had said his coming to see her had 'absolutely nothing to do with duty...'

'So.' Lily stood nervously in the middle of her small but cosy sitting room fifteen minutes later, very aware of him as he stood a few feet away from her.

The removal of his outer jacket a few minutes ago had revealed that he wore a black fitted cashmere sweater and faded jeans that rested low on the leanness of his hips, emphasising the long length of his legs; he obviously hadn't come to see her straight from a business meeting!

'Would you like a glass of red wine?' she asked self-consciously. 'It isn't anywhere near the calibre of the ones you have at the *palazzo,* but—'

'I would prefer a hot drink, if you don't mind,' Dmitri replied. 'Do you have any idea how cold it was,

waiting outside in the car park for you all that time?'
he added by way of explanation.

Lily's eyes widened. It had never occurred to her!
'How long were you waiting?'

He shrugged those wide shoulders. 'Felix told me
that you usually leave at about four-thirty, so I arrived
at four-fifteen just to err on the side of caution.'

Four-fifteen? Dmitri had been waiting outside for
her for over an hour and a half? He was right—that
didn't sound like the action of a man who had come to
see her out of a sense of duty... 'Why didn't you just
come inside and find me?'

He grimaced. 'I had no idea whether you would wish
to see me again at all—let alone at your place of work.'

'So you just waited?'

'Yes.'

'Why?'

Pale green eyes looked at her unblinkingly through
long dark lashes. 'Do you wish me to give you the socially polite answer or the truth?' he finally said huskily.

Lily looked amused. 'I don't think the two of us
have ever been socially polite to each other, have we?'

'No,' he accepted. 'But perhaps it is not too late for
us to start being so?'

Lily didn't want him to be polite to her. It was one of
the reasons, after all, that she had refused to attend the
Blessing in Rome on Saturday! The main one being, of
course, that she was wildly, deeply in love with him.

She moistened her lips before answering. 'Is that
what you want, Dmitri? For us to start being socially
polite to each other for Claudia and Felix's sake?'

No, it was not what he wanted at all! Being here with
Lily, talking with her again, seeing how beautiful she

looked in a dark blue sweater that matched the colour of her eyes, and black tailored trousers that clearly defined her curvaceous hips and bottom, told him just how much he *didn't* wish for social politeness between them—for Claudia and Felix's sake, or anyone else's!

His hands clenched at his sides. 'I will take that if it is all you have to give me, yes,' he said tensely.

She looked shocked. 'But it isn't what you really want?'

'No.'

A nerve pulsed at the base of her creamy throat. 'Then what *do* you want?'

He drew in a ragged breath. 'What do I want?' he repeated slowly, his smile self-derisive. 'Everything. I want everything, Lily,' he said. 'All that you are. Everything that you have to give.'

She gave a dazed shake of her head, her eyes wide. 'Are you saying that you want us to have an affair? That you would like to come here and spend the night with me whenever you happen to be in London on business?'

'No!' he exclaimed furiously. 'No, damn it, that is *not* what I am saying,' he reiterated, stepping forward to take a tight grasp of her arms. 'It sullies what I feel for you to even suggest I would treat you so casually!' He glared down at her.

She became very still. 'What you feel for me?' she whispered.

'You have no idea how I have longed to see you again these past two weeks, Lily. How every day without you has been a punishment. I am here now because I simply could not bear not seeing you again for one more day. It was not a business trip that brought me to England, Lily—only a desire, a longing, to see you. I flew to England today because Felix told me late last night that you were not coming to Italy at the weekend, as I had so hoped that you would.' His eyes glittered down at her.

Lily could barely breathe. She certainly couldn't take in, absorb, all the wonderful things Dmitri was saying to her. All that they implied...

'I am in love with you, Lily,' Dmitri stated. 'No—it is so much more than just love,' he declared. 'I adore everything about you. From the way that you look, your sense of humour, your fiery spirit, to the honourable and truthful person you are.' His voice gentled as he looked down at her hungrily. 'Making love with you was the most wonderful, satisfying experience of my life. Waking up in bed with you beside me—the first time that has ever happened with any woman,' he added firmly, 'was wondrous—a time I did not want to end.'

'And then you received Claudia's phone call.'

'And then I received that telephone call and behaved like an arrogant fool.' He gave a self-disgusted shake of his head. 'Lily, these past two weeks without you have made me realise that I wish to wake up with you in my arms every morning for the rest of my life. That I want to ask you to become my wife.'

'Dmitri!' she gasped, tears glistening in her eyes at the wonderful things he was saying to her.

'Please do not cry.' His expression was gentle as he smoothed those tears from her lashes. 'I only wish to tell you how I feel about you—not cause you any embarrassment or pain.' His hands slowly dropped back to her sides. 'I will go now—'

'You most certainly will not!' Lily told him forcefully.

Dmitri looked down at her quizzically. Hopefully. 'No?'

'Definitely no!' she instructed firmly. 'I've spent the past two weeks aching for you!'

His throat moved convulsively as he swallowed. 'You have?'

'Yes.' Lily stepped close to him and moved her arms up about his shoulders, her gaze steady as she looked into those beautiful pale green eyes. 'I fell in love with you in Rome, Dmitri,' she admitted. 'Completely head over heels in love with you!'

He looked down at her disbelievingly. 'But—'

'No buts, Dmitri.' She put gentle but silencing fingertips against the warmth of his lips. 'You are the reason I couldn't come back to Rome at the weekend—but only because I love you so much that just the thought of seeing you again, of having you treat me as no more than a passing acquaintance, was painful to me. I love you, Dmitri,' she breathed. 'I *love* you!'

'Bella cara!' Dmitri gathered her tightly into his arms, a look of wonder on those austere features as he gazed down at her. *'Mi amor! Mi—'*

'English, Dmitri,' she pleaded emotionally. 'I promise I will learn Italian soon, but at the moment I have no idea what it is you're saying to me.'

His eyes had darkened to emerald-green. 'I believe I would prefer to show you rather than tell you what you mean to me.'

Which Dmitri proceeded to do. Very thoroughly. Very convincingly. Until Lily was left in absolutely no doubt as to the love they felt for each other.

'Marry me, *cara!*' Dmitri urged huskily a long time later, as they lay nakedly entwined in each other's arms. 'Marry me, Lily, and one day we will both enjoy telling of our unconventional meeting to our grandchildren.'

Their grandchildren...

'Oh, yes, Dmitri. Yes!' Lily accepted gladly, having absolutely no doubt that her one night with an Italian count was going to last a lifetime.

* * * * *

You can find more information on upcoming Harlequin® titles, free excerpts and more at www.Harlequin.com.

HPCNM1112

REQUEST YOUR FREE BOOKS!

Harlequin *Presents*

PASSION
GUARANTEED
SEDUCTION

2 FREE NOVELS PLUS
2 FREE GIFTS!

YES! Please send me 2 FREE Harlequin Presents® novels and my 2 FREE gifts (gifts are worth about $10). After receiving them, if I don't wish to receive any more books, I can return the shipping statement marked "cancel." If I don't cancel, I will receive 6 brand-new novels every month and be billed just $4.30 per book in the U.S. or $4.99 per book in Canada. That's a saving of at least 14% off the cover price! It's quite a bargain! Shipping and handling is just 50¢ per book in the U.S. and 75¢ per book in Canada.* I understand that accepting the 2 free books and gifts places me under no obligation to buy anything. I can always return a shipment and cancel at any time. Even if I never buy another book, the two free books and gifts are mine to keep forever.

106/306 HDN FERQ

Name	(PLEASE PRINT)

Address	Apt. #

City	State/Prov.	Zip/Postal Code

Signature (if under 18, a parent or guardian must sign)

Mail to the **Reader Service:**
IN U.S.A.: P.O. Box 1867, Buffalo, NY 14240-1867
IN CANADA: P.O. Box 609, Fort Erie, Ontario L2A 5X3

Not valid for current subscribers to Harlequin Presents books.

**Are you a current subscriber to Harlequin Presents books
and want to receive the larger-print edition?
Call 1-800-873-8635 or visit www.ReaderService.com.**

* Terms and prices subject to change without notice. Prices do not include applicable taxes. Sales tax applicable in N.Y. Canadian residents will be charged applicable taxes. Offer not valid in Quebec. This offer is limited to one order per household. All orders subject to credit approval. Credit or debit balances in a customer's account(s) may be offset by any other outstanding balance owed by or to the customer. Please allow 4 to 6 weeks for delivery. Offer available while quantities last.

Your Privacy—The Reader Service is committed to protecting your privacy. Our Privacy Policy is available online at www.ReaderService.com or upon request from the Reader Service.

We make a portion of our mailing list available to reputable third parties that offer products we believe may interest you. If you prefer that we not exchange your name with third parties, or if you wish to clarify or modify your communication preferences, please visit us at www.ReaderService.com/consumerchoice or write to us at Reader Service Preference Service, P.O. Box 9062, Buffalo, NY 14269. Include your complete name and address.

HP11B

*Is the Santina-Jackson royal fairy-tale engagement
too good to be true?*

*Read on for a sneak peek of
PLAYING THE ROYAL GAME by USA TODAY
bestselling author Carol Marinelli.*

* * *

"I HAVE also spoken to my parents."

"They've heard?"

"They were the ones who alerted me!" Alex said. "We
have aides who monitor the press and the news constantly."
Did she not understand he had been up all night dealing
with this? "I am waiting for the palace to ring—to see how
we will respond."

She couldn't think, her head was spinning in so many
directions and Alex's presence wasn't exactly calming—
not just his tension, not just the impossible situation, but
the sight of him in her kitchen, the memory of his kiss. That
alone would have kept her thoughts occupied for days on
end, but to have to deal with all this, too…. And now the
doorbell was ringing. He followed her as she went to hit the
display button.

"It's my dad." She was actually a bit relieved to see him.
"He'll know what to do, how to handle—"

"I thought you hated scandal," Alex interrupted.

"We'll just say—"

"I don't think you understand." Again he interrupted
her and there was no trace of the man she had met yesterday; instead she faced not the man but the might of

Crown Prince Alessandro Santina. "There is no question that you will go through with this."

"You can't force me." She gave a nervous laugh. "We both know that yesterday was a mistake." She could hear the doorbell ringing. She went to press the intercom but his hand halted her, caught her by the wrist. She shot him the same look she had yesterday, the one that should warn him away, except this morning it did not work.

"You agreed to this, Allegra, the money is sitting in your account." He looked down at the paper. "Of course, we could tell the truth…" He gave a dismissive shrug. "I'm sure they have photos of later."

"It was just a kiss…."

"An expensive kiss," Alex said. "I wonder what the papers would make of it if they found out I bought your services yesterday."

"You wouldn't." She could see it now, could see the horrific headlines—she, Allegra, in the spotlight, but for shameful reasons.

"Oh, Allegra," he said softly but without endearment. "Absolutely I would. It's far too late to change your mind."

* * *

Pick up PLAYING THE ROYAL GAME by Carol Marinelli on November 13, 2012, from Harlequin® Presents®.

HARLEQUIN *Presents*

When legacy commands, these Greek royals must obey!

Discover a page-turning new Harlequin Presents®
duet from *USA TODAY* bestselling author

Maisey Yates

A ROYAL WORLD APART

Desperate to escape an arranged marriage, Princess
Evangelina has tried every trick in her little black book
to dodge her security guards. But where everyone else
has failed, will her new bodyguard bend her to his
will…and steal her heart?

Available November 13, 2012.

AT HIS MAJESTY'S REQUEST

Prince Stavros Drakos rules his country like his
business—with a will of iron! And when duty demands
an heir, this resolute bachelor will turn his sole
focus to the task….

But will he finally have met his match in a world-
renowned matchmaker?

**Coming December 18, 2012,
wherever books are sold.**

Harlequin *Desire*

ALWAYS POWERFUL, PASSIONATE AND PROVOCATIVE.

DON'T MISS THE SEDUCTIVE CONCLUSION TO THE MINISERIES

THE HIGHEST BIDDER

WITH FAN-FAVORITE AUTHOR

BARBARA DUNLOP

Prince Raif Khouri believes that Waverly's high-end-auction-house executive Ann Richardson is responsible for the theft of his valuable antique Gold Heart statue, rumored to be a good luck charm to his family. The only way Raif can keep an eye on her—and get the truth from her—is by kidnapping Ann and taking her to his kingdom. But soon Raif finds himself the prisoner as Ann tempts him like no one else.

A GOLDEN BETRAYAL

Available December 2012 from Harlequin® Desire.